NOT
FOR LOVE

NOT
FOR LOVE

HILA
COLMAN

William Morrow and Company
New York   1983

Printed in the United States of America.

10 9 8 7 6 5 4 3 2 1

Library of Congress Cataloging in Publication Data
Colman, Hila. Not for love.
   Summary: Sixteen-year-old Jill falls in love with a political activist and begins to experience some changing values.
   [1. Values—Fiction] I. Title. PZ7.C7No
1983   [Fic]   83-6120
ISBN 0-688-02419-X

For all of you:
Jennifer, Ethan, Ben, Sue, Jon, Sarah, and Jesse.
I'm counting on your generation to keep the peace.

CHAPTER
ONE

The day smelled of summer—of wild blackberries and cut grass, of thin cucumber sandwiches, damp bathing suits, and freshly ironed tennis shorts. The softness in the air spoke of brilliant, carefree days and the long, aimless evenings that spelled summer to a sixteen-year-old.

This summer, Jill thought, was going to be like all the others, except that it was going to be better. The first summer she would have her driver's license, and in the fall she would be a senior in high school. Her parents had decided that she should have this one last lazy vacation before she went to college.

Thinking about the coming summer as she walked the worn path that led from East Compton Senior High to the Compton Public Library, her books under her arm, Jill wondered why she didn't feel more exhilarated. Much as the thought of getting out of school only six or seven weeks from that May day thrilled her, she felt an uneasy sense of something missing. The feeling was not entirely new. It had in fact hit her a few times since Christmas vacation, and when she thought about it, Jill could almost pinpoint her first awareness of it to a day and a time.

She remembered shivering on the school steps one cold January morning watching a chartered bus fill up with a group of students from a political-science class. Wrapped in their parkas, heavy sweaters, and scarves, they were a pink-cheeked, laughing group exuding a kind of excitement that made Jill feel at that moment a dull emptiness about the day ahead of her: the usual classes, perhaps spending the afternoon with her friend Diane Center, perhaps shopping with her mother. . . . For a few moments she saw her life stretching ahead of her in a bleak series of days like those of her friends' mothers—shopping, cooking meals, taking care of a husband, wiping their children's noses. It had been windy standing there, and Jill recalled pulling her down coat tighter around her; but still she did not go inside.

The bus was marked "Washington, D.C." "What are you going to do there?" Jill had asked Toby Wells, a boy whom she recognized as a political activist, a leader in practically all the school dissident groups. He had led the fight to keep students from being suspended for absenteeism, he had started a debating club, and he was famous for having once been arrested in New Hampshire, together with a lot of other people, in an antinuclear demonstration. His name was often in the High School News column in the weekly East Compton newspaper.

Toby's intense gray-green eyes were almost green in

2

the bright sunshine, and his silly red wool cap did not contain his thick, unruly black hair. "We're going to meet with our congressman and sit in at Congress," he said, grinning. "See our great democracy at work. Want to come? We have a few extra seats."

"Oh, no, that's not my thing. I hate politics, it's boring."

Toby's eyes held hers. She could feel him taking in her long auburn-blonde hair, her slim figure perhaps a head shorter than his. She had kept looking at him until she lowered her own dark-blue eyes, willing him to admire her thick, curly lashes. She was not going to be intimidated by the power of his self-assurance, but neither was she prepared for his serious voice.

"You only say that because you don't know," he had said gently, as if he were talking to someone he had known for a long time. "Everything you do, the very air you breathe depends on politics. This school, how much you paid for the coat you're wearing, what you put on your face."

"I don't put anything on my face," Jill had said with a laugh, wishing he wasn't talking to her as if she were his kid sister. He couldn't be more than eighteen himself.

"You don't have to," he said. "It's quite all right the way it is."

"I didn't think you'd notice anything as unimportant as a girl's face," she said mockingly.

Toby had laughed. "You have me down as a weirdo, don't you?"

"Are you?"

The bus driver called out that the bus was leaving in a few minutes. Toby turned away with a nod goodbye. Jill had stood watching until the bus drove off. She had waved goodbye, and thought she saw Toby at a window waving to her.

She waited until the bus was out of sight, somewhat alarmed by the surge of elation that replaced her earlier depression. The very fact that Toby had stopped to talk to her, had invited her to go on the trip, made her feel there could be a lot about herself she had not yet discovered.

Jill had never thought about herself very deeply, nor taken herself seriously. She had always thought of herself as someone who would be carefree and young for a long time. Darker thoughts of an unknown future, or one that she saw in bleak colors, were momentary and soon dismissed. She had more or less taken for granted that, yes, someday she would have a profession, someday she would get married; but since she had not yet chosen what that career was going to be, nor fallen deeply in love, she lived in a lighthearted present. The future would take care of itself.

She was not unfeeling or shallow, but rather a girl whose emotions had not yet been tapped by any great personal experience. However, she was ready and eager to open her heart and mind to the world. When a classmate's family had lost their belongings in a fire, Jill had been the first to empty her closet and take some of her clothes over to them. She had done it quietly, without even consulting her parents, not aware of doing anything special. Her schoolmate's gratitude had only embarrassed her. She cared about people and assumed everyone else did; but Toby's way of caring in an organized way for the world in general, rather than individuals, was a new thought for her. A stimulating thought.

When she had seen Toby around school after that day and they passed each other in the cafeteria or the halls, she felt flustered and would say something meaningless like, "How's the real world doing?" and he would answer with something equally inane. Once he asked, "You still hate politics?"

"I don't feel strongly enough to hate," she had answered foolishly.

Yet the vague uneasiness—a sense of other people, kids her own age, having a direction, a purpose in their lives that she did not have—remained. They shared an excitement perhaps that came from things she didn't know about. She had taken to reading different books, not just the mystery and romance stories she read in bed at night. She took books from the library about the Great Depression, like John Steinbeck's *Grapes of Wrath*; she read books about the Second World War and the horrors of German concentration camps. She found herself becoming interested in books about courage and dedication to strong and sometimes unpopular beliefs. She was upset by tales of life in India and Africa and of how people had to struggle just to get enough to eat to stay alive. She thought a lot about her own country, the American Revolution and the Civil War, the civil-rights battles of the sixties, and she was surprised by how little she knew of the world outside of her own town of East Compton, and the sacrifices people made for their principles.

Yet she stayed away from the group of students her father called "troublemakers," the ones who raised a fuss when the school board removed *Catcher in the Rye* and two books by Kurt Vonnegut from the school library. When some members of the same group picketed a nuclear power plant on the outskirts of town, Jill somehow never got around to signing a petition that they circulated.

As she approached the library that May day, she didn't feel like going inside. She was not in the mood for reading nor for the quiet, scholarly, old-leather smell of the small building, discreetly marked BUILT 1920 in its cornerstone. Nor did she want to think about politics. The day was one for lying in a hammock, or stretched out in the sun to start ridding herself of the pallid winter whiteness of her skin.

Standing ahead of her at the desk for returning books was Toby Wells. Dressed in an open-necked shirt, with no sweater or jacket, he looked as if summer had already arrived.

He gave her a wide smile, and frankly looked to see the

titles of the books she was returning. "I thought you didn't like politics," he said, reading the title of a biography of Franklin Delano Roosevelt.

"It was for a social-studies class," Jill said, irritated that she sounded apologetic. Inexplicably, she didn't want him to learn of her recent change in reading tastes, nor the fact that he was the one who had inspired it. She felt embarrassed with him, as if her having thought about him so much since that cold January day, admiring him and at the same time resenting his intrusion into the calm, uneventful days of her life, gave him a power over her.

"It's a very good book," Toby said.

"I found it interesting," she said truthfully.

He gave her a curious glance. "Why do you like to play dumb?"

"I'm not playing. I am dumb. A dumb blonde." Her eyes were laughing at him.

"I'll bet. What are you going to take out now?"

"I don't know. Something dumb and sexy. Can you recommend anything? No, I guess not. You wouldn't read anything like that. It would be beneath you."

"You're right, I won't deny it. I don't waste my time on trash." Toby's gray-green eyes were holding hers.

"You mean like me?"

"No, I don't mean like you. If you consider yourself trash then you are stupid. And I don't think you are."

Jill kept her eyes on his unflinching. "No, I don't consider myself trash," she said quietly.

"Want to go for a walk?" he asked abruptly.

She was surprised and flustered. "We'd have to carry books."

"No, we can come back later. The library's open till nine tonight."

"Okay, it would be nice. It's a beautiful day."

She didn't ask where they were going, she simply went along with him, and wasn't surprised when he led the way to an ice-skating pond away from the village. The trees had begun to leaf, and a few early dogwood blossoms showed in the woods. Some of the lawns they passed were bordered with bright forsythia.

Jill did not try to make light conversation. She felt good just walking alongside Toby, flattered in a special way that he had asked her. She was used to male attention. Being a very pretty, animated girl, she received more phone calls than her parents liked; yet being with Toby was different. He was a brain, he did things, she was sure that fantastic thoughts went on in his head, and he was not afraid to stand up for what he thought was right. In another age, Jill thought romantically, he might have been a martyr, someone who went to the gallows, saying until his death, "The earth is round."

Their conversation was not world-shaking. They talked about school, about some movies they'd both seen, and about their favorite records. "I didn't think you'd be into jazz or punk rock," Jill said as they neared the end of their turn around the water. "I thought you'd only like classical."

"I like a lot of things," Toby said. "I'm very open. Except when it comes to politics. I'll listen to all sides but I'm not open to reactionaries and bigots. When it comes to survival," he said with a grin, "I definitely have a point of view. I'm for it."

"Politics isn't exactly a question of life and death," Jill said. "It seems to me it doesn't make any difference whether one person is elected or another. It doesn't affect you or me."

"That is where you are wrong." Toby took her arm to keep her from stepping into a hole in the road. "Remember, I told you once that politics affects everything in your life. Not only Congress but dozens of government agencies do. And now, more than ever, who's elected can affect whether you live or die. You heard of Three Mile Island, didn't you? And Indian Point? How do you like the idea of a nuclear plant being built, right here, within a few miles of East Compton, where we live?"

Jill shrugged. "I'm not going to worry about it. There's nothing we can do anyway. I imagine they know what they're doing. No one's out to endanger our lives."

"That's what you think. I don't believe anyone is deliberately setting out to kill us, they just ignore certain facts they don't want to know about and rationalize what they are doing. They say we need the power, that it's all very safe, that the chance of an accident is nil; but the engineers and the doctors know better. The truth is that one small accident can kill thousands."

"You sound very sure of yourself." Jill turned her

deep-blue eyes on him. "What makes you right and the others wrong?"

"It's not just my personal opinion. I've read a lot about it, I know about the accidents that haven't been publicized. No one has figured out yet how to dispose of radioactive waste. In this country a full-scale storage crisis is expected by 1990, and I don't want to just sit around and wait for that to happen. It's insane to build more nuclear plants when there's no safe way to dispose of the nuclear waste we already have. People don't want a dump site in their backyards."

Jill turned away from Toby to look at the water. She was afraid her face would give her away, would reveal to him how electrified she was by his enthusiasm, the light in his eyes when he spoke. She could listen to him forever. That he was only a boy, not yet nineteen, did not matter. She was proud that she was walking with someone who she felt was going to do important things.

"Am I boring you?" Toby asked.

"No, of course not. It's fascinating—and frightening." She sighed. "It must be wonderful to feel so strongly about something. Like being religious. I envy people who are deeply religious; it must be very comforting."

"Don't you feel deeply about anything?" Toby looked at her, his gleaming eyes squinting in the bright sunshine.

Jill flushed. She was embarrassed. He made her feel ashamed of the things that were important to her—like terribly wanting a new tennis racket, or saving her money to visit a girlfriend who had moved to London with her family. Perhaps most of all of wanting so much to fall in love. She was sure Toby would think all of those things were silly. "I guess I do care," she said, "but about different things. I feel deeply about people, I think."

"People are important, the most important," Toby replied.

They walked in silence. Jill wanted to know so many things about him that she would never ask: Did he have a girl? Had he ever been in love? She even felt shy about asking him if he was going in for politics as a profession for fear he might think she was asking prying questions. She hated it when people, mainly her parents' friends, asked what she was planning to do when she got out of school. They made her feel that she should say something significant, like being a doctor or a physicist, when in fact she hadn't even decided about college.

"You make me feel unimportant," Jill said as they began to go around the pond a second time. "As if I'm wasting my time."

Toby laughed. "Everyone's important. But maybe you are wasting your time. You don't have to. There's lots to do."

"Like what?"

"Well, there's going to be a big demonstration against the new plant on June first. You must have seen posters around. You can start by coming to that."

"If I saw posters I didn't pay attention. Going to a demonstration doesn't seem like anything much to do. I'd just be another body there."

"That's exactly what we need. Lots and lots of bodies. A small turnout wouldn't mean much, but if hundreds of people came, we'd carry weight. I think you'd find it exciting."

"Is that what you are looking for—excitement?" For the first time she had the courage to question him.

He flushed. "No, although it is exciting. I want to change things, I want to be a force in changing the world."

She almost smiled. "That's awfully ambitious. What makes you think you will make it any better? Just changing isn't enough. Hitler wanted to change his world too, but we wouldn't have liked what he made of it, would we?"

"Certainly not. That's the point. I don't want power as an individual, but I believe in people power. I don't want my life to depend on the whims of one man, or a few men in power. Not an American president nor a Russian one."

"But it doesn't," Jill said mildly. "You just said that Congress affects my life. Well, all those senators and congressmen and women were elected by people, some of them the same people who are demonstrating. There's no one person making decisions."

"But the people have to let the men and women they elected know what they want. That's what it's all about. You can't just go to the polls and vote and then forget about it. I don't want nuclear plants because they are dangerous, and I don't want a nuclear war because it would destroy the planet. It's that simple."

"I don't think it's simple," Jill said, daring to disagree with him. "I think it's very complicated because we can't do it by ourselves, and the people who are building the nuclear plant are more powerful than we are. To stop them will be very hard."

"But don't you think it's worth a try?" Toby turned around to look her full in the face, and she thought she saw a spark of admiration in his eyes.

"It's worth trying if you believe you can win," she said.

He shook his head impatiently. "No, you're wrong. You have to try and keep trying, *until* you win. Will you come to the demonstration?" She felt that he was asking her more than that one question, and that her answer was going to be more of a commitment than simply a yes about the demonstration.

"I'll have to think about it," she said, and she really intended to.

After they completed their second turn around the water, they walked back to the library. Jill wished the walk wasn't ending, and that she could think of some way to have them meet again, not just in school but on a date. She had never felt so self-conscious before with a boy. Usually she was relaxed and carefree—if a boy liked her, okay, and if he didn't that was his problem. Toby was different. She wanted to touch his curly hair tumbling almost to his shoulders, she wanted to feel the strength of his arms around her. She wanted to be important to him, to have him look at her with that direct gaze of his and have his eyes light up the way he did when he spoke about the things he believed in. She wanted him to believe in her.

They each got their books and parted casually, with a brief "See you around." Jill walked home feeling a heaviness that she knew wasn't from the books she was carrying. She felt as if she had said goodbye to someone very special. As much as she told herself she was silly, he was someone she hardly knew, she couldn't rid herself of the feeling of desolation. In her mind Toby was a shining knight who was riding off to conquer the world and had left her behind. That is, unless she joined him. The thought lifted her spirits.

CHAPTER
TWO

J ill lived with her parents in a modest ranch house that
was part of a development built some ten years earlier.
Jill, who had lived in East Compton since she was three
years old, could remember playing in the woods where
her house now stood. She had been furious when the
bulldozers had come in and cut down the big tree she used
to sit under and play "make-believe." But what had once
been barren houses, looking as if they would blow away
with the wind, were now settled in with landscaped
lawns, gardens, trees, and bushes.

Jill's spirits rose a little as she approached her house.
She thought her parents had picked a choice spot. Their
house was on top of a small rise with the lawn curving
down to a minute stream. While the white house with its
black shutters had no distinctive architecture, it sat solidly
on its foundation and by now looked as if it had been
there for a long time.

She was not surprised to see her mother absorbed in

pruning a small crab-apple tree in front of the screened porch. Mrs. Simon was a tall, angular woman whose graying hair and weather-beaten face made her look older than her years, in spite of her bright-blue eyes, a shade lighter than Jill's. She spent her winters poring over seed catalogs and at the first hint of spring was outdoors digging and planting.

"I'm not going to let that guy spoil my summer," Jill thought as if the house, with her mother in front, were assuring her that she had a good life and she should enjoy it. Let those who wanted to worry about a nuclear disaster that was unlikely to happen anyway. Who would be fool enough to start a nuclear war? As for accidents in nuclear plants—well, there were always accidents everywhere, and Jill didn't think anyone could stop them.

"Hi, Mom," she said, stopping to watch her mother's absorbed face. Even she had something she was deeply involved in. Maybe deciding whether to enlarge the peony bed or to put in more dahlias wasn't earthshaking, but gardening kept her mother interested and active.

"I think I'd like to get a few more fruit trees," Mrs. Simon said, stepping back to admire the tree she'd been working on. "They are so satisfactory. Lovely to look at and giving you fruit. Perhaps a peach tree and a couple of small cherry trees. What do you think?"

"That sounds nice." Jill nodded in agreement. Her feelings for her mother shifted frequently, probably, Jill suspected, depending on her own mood. A good deal of the time she felt sorry for her parent, sensing that she was filling up empty holes with her passion for her garden. Other times she admired her for her persistence. And yet, occasionally, Jill wished her mother was more accessible. She never felt that she could talk to her about her own feelings, her need to be loved, to fall in love, her physical desires—it was hard to imagine that tall, somewhat remote, preoccupied woman ever being in love. And yet why else would she have married Jill's father?

It was Mrs. Simon's Danish father, Grandpa Nilsen, a dairy farmer in Wisconsin, who had had the money. Jill had heard the story of how her father, who had grown up a poor boy in New Hampshire, had hitchhiked out west one summer while he was still in college and gotten a temporary job haying on the Nilsen farm. That was when her parents had fallen in love.

Later her mother had come east and they had gotten married. They had lived with her father's parents until Jill was three. Then they had moved to Massachusetts and bought their present house. Her father had earned a degree in business and his first job had been in a bank. Little by little he had been promoted, and now he was an officer in a reputable but small commercial bank.

Jill suspected that her mother's marriage had been a disappointment. Whatever promise of adventure Mrs. Simon had envisioned when she became attracted to the young, handsome eastern boy had probably faded over the years. With each promotion Jill believed her father had become more conservative, more anxious to hobnob with the "right" people, more fixed in his thinking and his ways. Her mother's response had been to grow more within herself, and sometimes Jill wondered if the two ever really talked to each other. They didn't even fight. Everything was smooth and harmonious, but often Jill longed to hear the quiet broken with a voice screaming, or a door being slammed. She wanted a sign of emotion, of life.

When she left her mother and went up to her room, Jill thought that control, that absence of any show of feelings in her own house, was one reason she found Toby so attractive. She envied his intensity, his enthusiasm, and the excitement he generated. That was what she wanted in her own life, but she had not understood until now her own restlessness and the sense of something missing. She wanted to feel deeply, passionately, to live life to its fullest even if it hurt. She felt ready for something tremendous to happen to her.

As Jill stood alongside the freshly starched white bedroom window curtains, she could see her mother bending over a flower bed along the driveway to the garage. Jill involuntarily shook her head in wonder at how little her mother knew about her daughter's life. She had not even asked where she had been that afternoon. Mrs. Simon would placidly go on working in her garden, totally unaware that her only child had had a great experience. Had, in fact, fallen in love.

In a way this lack of closeness was a relief. Not having someone want to understand her had its advantages. Although Jill often felt lonely, it was easier, and safer, to keep her shifting emotions to herself. She had no idea of what went on in her mother's head, but Jill was sure she would never in a million years understand her daughter's passionate urges, her sexual fantasies, nor even her intellectual need to do something important.

That evening at the dinner table, Jill felt compelled to bring Toby into the conversation. Her mind was so full of him she couldn't contain herself. She spoke as casually as she could. "A boy in our school, Toby Wells, was telling me about a demonstration on June first against the nuclear plant. He's terribly excited about it and asked me if I'd like to go to it."

Her father stopped cutting his meat and put down his knife and fork. "Toby Wells? I know all about him. He's a good person for you to stay away from." Mr. Simon's handsome face had a fleeting look of contempt, as if he were talking about some scum, and Jill's heart sank.

"What do you know about him? He's a very bright, nice boy." She would never let either of her parents know how much Toby affected her.

"I know enough, and from a very good source, his own father." He gave Jill a smug smile. "I play golf with him. Henry Wells is a decent man and a pretty good player. He's trying to get that B & J Manufacturing plant back on its feet. He's a crackerjack engineer but in this economy I don't know if he can put that place back in the black. Anyway, he and his wife are plenty troubled about their son. Don't get mixed up with him, he's a bad lot."

"I don't believe it. What's wrong with him, just tell me one thing." Jill knew she was getting more excited than she should, but she couldn't help it.

"He's a troublemaker, plain and simple. Demonstrating against that plant, bah! That nuclear plant's the best thing to happen around here in years. Gives people jobs, provides power we need badly. We need to build up industry and industry needs power. East Compton would be a ghost town in ten years without that plant. Don't forget I'm in the bank, I can see what's happening."

"According to Toby we could all be ghosts, dead ones, if that plant had an accident. You should hear what he has to say."

"I think your father knows what he's talking about," Mrs. Simon said mildly. Her mother had such a faraway expression on her face that Jill hadn't been sure she'd been listening.

"Maybe," Jill said with a deceptive meekness. What was the point of defending Toby, she thought, when she'd probably never hear from him anyway? She'd only go to the demonstration, she decided, if he did call her or asked her for a date when they met in school.

She had a feeling that if he was going to call her, he'd call that night, as an aftermath of their walk. If Toby felt at all the way she did, he'd have to call. But the evening passed and the only phone call was for her mother from the Garden Club.

Jill waited until eleven o'clock to go up to bed, annoyed with herself for being such a fool. Why on earth would a boy like Toby call someone like herself? He probably thought she was the dumbest girl he'd ever met.

The next morning, however, Jill chose her clothes for school carefully, and fussed with her hair for so long she came close to missing her bus. Toby was outside with a group of boys and girls when she got off the bus. He waved to her but didn't leave his friends. Jill hurried past them into the building, silently cursing herself, Toby, and everyone connected with antinuclear demonstrations. She had especially dire thoughts for one girl in particular, Pat Foner, a tall, dark-haired, striking girl who had been standing with her arm on Toby's shoulder. They had looked stunning together, and Jill was sure the other girl was well aware of it. Pat was involved in all the same things as Toby, and while Pat was supposed to have a boyfriend who was a freshman in college, Jill suspected that she wasn't just sitting home on the weekends.

"You look dark and angry," Jill's friend, Diane Center, greeted her.

Jill faced Diane and again marveled to herself at how fashionably she was dressed. Diane's French mother was a fine dressmaker who designed and made clothes for the wealthier suburbanites. Diane had inherited her mother's distinctively European looks together with her shrewd mind and fine style. Jill was constantly awed by Diane's ability to wear the most ordinary dress or slacks and with a scarf or a string of beads manage to look chic. That day she had tied a red cummerbund over her blue jeans and with it wore a frilly white blouse. The result was stunning.

"I'm really not," Jill replied, then shrugged with a helpless gesture. "Well, maybe I am. If I'm angry it's only at myself. I'm not very bright."

"What made you come to that conclusion?"

"I'll tell you at lunch. Got to go to my class now," Jill said, getting some books out of her locker and walking away.

Jill was glad that she had lab that morning as biology was her favorite subject. She had been doing some experiments with white mice, and she spent an absorbing hour compiling her data so that later she could feed it into the school computer. The morning flew by and when Jill went to meet Diane in the school cafeteria for lunch, she had quite forgotten her earlier gloom.

After the girls had gotten their lunch trays and found a quiet corner table, Diane said, "So tell me, why were you angry?"

Jill laughed. "Did I look so mad? I wasn't really; more annoyed. With myself. I let myself be carried away for twenty-four hours. I'm over it now."

But no sooner had she said the words than she looked up straight into the gray-green eyes of Toby Wells, who was carrying his tray past their table. Her heart gave a great swoop, and she knew her words were a big fake.

"Hi," Toby said. "How you doing?"

"Fine." She was tongue-tied for a few seconds. "You know Diane, don't you?" she said stiffly.

"Sure, we see each other around," Toby said amiably. Then, looking directly at Jill, he added, "We'll have to go for another walk one of these days."

"That would be nice," Jill said, feeling that she sounded prim.

"What was that all about?" Diane asked after Toby had left them. "I never saw you act that way."

"What way? Did I sound stupid?"

Diane looked at her friend in amazement. "Not stupid," she said slowly, "just kind of self-conscious. Like you'd never talked to a boy before in your life. And I know better," she added with a giggle. "I mean, you're a pretty sophisticated girl but you acted like you were about ten years old. What's going on?"

Jill shook her head despairingly. "He makes me feel that way. He's so, I don't know. . . . I think he's wonderful, don't you?" she said suddenly.

Diane laughed. "Was that your twenty-four-hour romance? If you ask me, from the way you behaved just now, it's going to go on for a lot more than twenty-four hours."

"I doubt it." Jill smiled ruefully. "I wish my face didn't give me away so much. Anyway, he doesn't give a hang about me—he's all politics. Except maybe for Pat Foner." She glanced over to a table where Toby was sitting with a group that included Pat.

"I don't think so. I think he's available, and I bet anything you'll hear from him."

"Do you think so?" Jill's voice was eager. Then she

shook her head again. "I doubt it. I'm not a brain."

"You may be dumb, but you sure are pretty." A boy's voice behind her made Jill jump. She turned around to see Dwight Armstrong standing in back of her chair.

"Oh, you. Thanks a lot."

"You know I don't mean it," Dwight said with a grin.

"Which, that I'm not dumb or that I'm not pretty?" Jill asked.

"I think you're brilliant and beautiful. Don't you agree?" he turned to Diane, and then sat himself down at their table.

"She's not my type," Diane said teasingly. "I've got to go. I'll leave you two to fight it out."

Jill sat back and looked at Dwight. He was not handsome, but he had a good, even an interesting, face with bushy eyebrows and deep-set, somewhat dreamy eyes. His nose was slightly crooked, but rather than detract from his looks, this irregularity gave his face a certain strength that was substantiated by a firm chin. Jill liked Dwight and she knew that he was crazy about her. But she wished that he could make her heart race; and not for the first time, she wondered about the chemistry between people, especially those of the opposite sex.

"What you thinking of?" Dwight asked.

"I'm thinking I really want to have a good time this summer. I can't wait to get out of school." As she spoke, Jill was looking past Dwight to the table where Toby was sitting next to Pat Foner.

Dwight followed her eyes. "You wouldn't have a good time with that bunch," he said.

Jill glanced at him, startled that he could read her thoughts. "I wasn't planning to," she replied.

"You want to go hear the Comets play tonight?"

"Oh, where are they playing?"

"At the Pub. I'll pick you up at seven-thirty, okay?"

"Sure, super."

Jill sat at the table alone when Dwight had to leave to make a class. She had a free period so she wasn't in a hurry. She was glancing over the notes from her morning classes and was surprised to see Pat Foner approach her table.

"Hi." Pat gave her a friendly smile. "Mind if I sit down?"

"No, of course not." Jill looked at her questioningly.

"Toby said you might be interested in going to our demonstration. That would be great, but it isn't for a few weeks. In the meantime we're showing an antinuke film and having a little party next Friday night. We thought you might like to come and find out more about what we're doing. Also meet the others. There's no charge but we will pass around the hat—just to cover expenses and to help defray the costs of the flyers and posters for the June demonstration. Will you come?"

"It sounds interesting," Jill said hesitatingly. She kept wondering why Toby hadn't come over to ask her himself.

"I think it will be. It's going to be in the Congregational Church's meeting hall. Friday night at seven-thirty. Please try to make it." Pat stood up and gave Jill a warm smile. "I'll look for you there."

Jill watched the girl wave and give a little nod to Toby and the others at his table before she walked out of the cafeteria. She wondered what Pat would later report back to them: "Let's work on her" or "She's pretty indifferent, we're wasting our time"?

Jill felt uncomfortable. She could already see the trap she was falling into. If Toby ever showed any signs of interest, she'd never know if he was nice to her because he wanted her to join their group or because he liked her for herself. With Pat she had clearly felt that in spite of the girl's friendly smiles, she was interested only in another recruit. Otherwise she probably wouldn't give Jill Simon the time of day.

"Well," Jill thought ruefully, "if they only want me as another demonstrator, I can do the same. I can go along with their politics because I'm interested in Toby. Tit for tat." She was amused by her plan although not exactly happy since then she would never know Toby's real feelings.

Jill gathered up her papers and books, and without turning her eyes toward Toby, she left for the study hall.

CHAPTER
THREE

Jill sat in her room watching the injured chipmunk she had found in the woods scamper around the cage Dwight had helped her to build. She had cared for Heloise, as she had named the animal, for four weeks now, and took delight in its health and energy. "I know I should let you go," Jill said to the bright-eyed little face, "but I like you too much. You're my friend. I'd be lonesome without you, and out in the woods you could get hurt again."

She leaned forward in her chair, and her voice became solemn. "There's a big world out there, Heloise, and it's scary. You and I are just tiny nothings. Toby says that if they build that power plant we are going to live in constant danger. Do you believe him? Do you think our government would allow that to happen? But Toby is so sure, and so sincere. And he is so good-looking. Do you think Toby ever cares about girls? He looks as if he might...." Jill sat back and sighed. "I'm stupid. I'm going out with Dwight tonight and I should be washing my hair and making myself pretty instead of talking to you. Don't stand on your head, Heloise, that's silly."

Jill tried to psych herself up into feeling enthusiastic about Dwight: he was a nice person, not an airhead, and super when surfing. He'd told her often she was foxy (his word for sexy), but he didn't make her feel that way. Something was missing. Now try as she would to convince herself he had it all, Toby's gray-green eyes kept popping into her mind.

Dwight had a surprise when he came to pick her up. "Come outside and you'll see," he said, when he'd come into the house and was chatting with her parents.

"Give me a hint," Jill said.

"Nothing doing. Just come out and you'll see."

"I think I can guess," Jill said, but she didn't say anything more.

In front of the house stood a slightly battered yellow VW convertible. "It's terrific." She gave Dwight a hug. "Sensational. When did you get it?"

"Today. It's not new, about seven years old, but I can fix it up. I'm going to give it a new coat of paint, and I have some work to do on the motor. I got a terrific buy, even my father said so. I haven't paid for it all yet, but my dad lent me some of the money. Do you like it?" Dwight's eyes were shining with pride.

"Like it? I love it. It's fantastic. You must be thrilled."

"I am. Come on, get in." Dwight opened the door for her. "Do you mind having the top down? I mean you don't care if you get blown around a bit?"

"Of course not. I adore a convertible."

On their ride to the Pub Dwight talked about all the things they could do that summer. Jill listened to his low, excited voice rattle off plans to drive them to the ocean, some fifty miles away, to go to an antique-car museum, to drive over to the Appalachian Trail and go hiking, to just drive and drive. "You have your license now, you can do some of the driving too. It's going to be terrific, Jill, isn't it?" He took one hand off the wheel and squeezed her arm. "No more asking if I can get my mom's car. I can't wait for summer, can you?"

"No, it's going to be great." Dwight flashed her a sidelong glance, and she smiled weakly. She knew her voice had sounded flat. "It's really going to be super," she added, forcing a brighter smile.

She was glad they didn't have to talk during the concert, and she was able to sit back in her seat and enjoy the music. She ignored Dwight's arm that had slid around her shoulder, and willed herself not to think about Toby because that would not be nice while Dwight was taking her out.

But after the set, when Dwight ordered sodas and hamburgers, he looked at her with a quizzical expression. "What's the matter? You seem far away tonight."

Jill shook her head. "I'm not. Maybe I'm tired."

"Maybe, but I think there's something else. You don't want to talk about it?"

"There's nothing to talk about." Another silence followed. After they had been served their food and drinks, Jill said, "Do you know anything about the demonstration they're having against the nuclear plant?"

Dwight shrugged. "Not much. I stay away from Toby Wells and Pat Foner and that crew. They're too serious, not my type. They're not going to change anything anyhow. I'd rather be surfing."

"I know what you mean." Jill nibbled at her hamburger and played with the pepper shaker. "Are Toby and Pat a couple?" she asked casually.

Dwight gave her a shrewd look. "I wouldn't know. Why?" he asked with a laugh.

"No reason." Jill laughed with him. "Just curious."

Dwight was still laughing. "You are the world's worst liar. I can see through you like a piece of glass. You have a crush on Toby."

"Don't be silly. I hardly know him. But Pat invited me to go see an antinuke film at the Congregational Church. Want to go?"

"No, thank you. You can go. They'll scare the hell out of you about the bomb; but bombs exist, and more power plants will get built, and no one's going to stop it."

"You're probably right." But Jill wished she had better answers for Dwight; she wasn't convinced he was right, and if Toby had been there, she thought, he'd have known what to say. She picked up her hamburger to finish it, and took a big bite. Her teeth clamped down on something much harder than any chopped meat, and gagging a little, Jill pulled a small hairpin out of her mouth. "Good God, look what was in my hamburger." She felt sick and quickly held a paper napkin close to her mouth to get rid of what she had not swallowed.

"Take some water, here." Dwight leaned over and held a glass to her mouth. "Drink it slowly."

Jill obeyed gratefully. "Isn't that awful?" she gasped. "I could have choked on it."

"I'm going to call the manager." Dwight stood up. "They're not going to get away with this."

"What's the use? Probably the cook's hairpin accidentally fell in. After all, nothing really happened to me." Jill couldn't bear scenes.

"You can't just let something like this go by. I won't." Dwight strode over to the cashier's desk, and Jill saw him talking earnestly, and rather angrily, with the manager. He had the hairpin with him. Soon the two of them came back to their table. Dwight had a smug grin on his face and the bald-headed man with him was all apology.

"Such a thing happening," the manager said to Jill. "In all my years in business, nothing like this ever happened. You want another hamburger? Order anything you want, on the house. Please excuse such a terrible thing. . . ."

"It's all right. Thank you, I don't think I want anything more."

"You sure? Maybe a steak, some french fries? It'll make you feel better."

"No, thanks very much. I'm not hungry."

The man looked at her beseechingly. "Will you forgive a little accident?"

"Yes, of course. I'm okay." She turned to Dwight. "Let's go."

The manager bowed them out.

"I guess it's a good thing you spoke up," Jill said, when they got into Dwight's car. "At least you didn't have to pay."

"You bet I didn't. That man was scared stiff you were going to sue." Dwight laughed. "He was really nervous."

"You see, it is good to speak up. You're the one who said it doesn't do any good. Maybe Toby and his friends are right."

"That's different." Dwight spoke a little impatiently. "One has nothing to do with the other."

"But they do. If you just keep quiet, nothing happens. You just proved that."

"You're making a ridiculous connection. That little hairpin could have choked you to death."

"What do you think an accident in a nuclear plant would do?"

Dwight gave her a disgusted look. "Honestly, Jill, I don't care."

When he parked the car in front of her house, Dwight took her in his arms and kissed her firmly on the mouth.

"If you think you're going to dump me for Toby Wells, you've got another think coming. I won't let you."

"Toby Wells doesn't mean a thing to me," Jill lied glibly. However she gently pushed Dwight away. "I am tired," she said. "And I still feel a little sick. I'd better go in." She kissed him good night and went into her dark house, up the stairs past the closed door of her parents' room, and into her own. She had left a small lamp on, and her room looked warm and welcoming.

Quickly she threw her clothes on a chair and got into bed. She wanted to think about Toby before she fell asleep, but her eyes closed, and the next thing she knew the sun was streaming into her window on the following bright spring morning.

The Congregational Church, off Main Street in the village, always looked as if its white facade had been freshly painted. It stood with the same simple dignity as the austere, taciturn men who had built it. As she stood in front of the church and saw only a few cars in the adjacent parking area, Jill thought that she might not go in. The church seemed so sturdy and peaceful; and having existed for almost a hundred years, surely it would still be there for another hundred. To go in there to see a film about the bomb seemed ridiculous. Yet Jill had known from the minute Pat had asked her that nothing would have kept her away if there was a chance to see Toby.

"I'm so glad you came," Pat Foner greeted her. She too

glanced at the parking area. "It's such a nice evening maybe a lot of people will walk." Pat smiled cheerfully. "Here's hoping. Come on, let's go in." Taking Jill's arm with a friendly gesture, Pat led her to a wing added on to the original building and into a large, well-lit room.

There were more people standing around in small groups, talking, than the few cars would have indicated. Jill was surprised by the mixture of young and old, and there were some among the older people whom she never would have expected to see at such a meeting. She recognized one woman who worked in the bank with her father. The woman looked at Jill with surprise, then came over and introduced herself. "I'm Sally Johnson, and you're Mr. Simon's daughter, aren't you? What does your father think of your being here?"

Jill gave an embarrassed laugh. "He doesn't know. I'll tell him later," she added.

Sally Johnson laughed. "I won't tell on you if you don't tell on me. What I do on my own time is none of the bank's business."

"No, of course not." Out of the corner of her eye, Jill spotted Toby over at a table covered with various pieces of literature. She turned from Ms. Johnson, and her eyes met Toby's. He beckoned her to come over. By this time Pat had left her to go into a kitchen where some girls were fixing coffee and arranging cookies and cakes on platters.

"Welcome," Toby greeted her. "I'm glad you made it."

"I am too." She still felt self-conscious with him. His eyes seemed to her slightly mocking, but not in a way to put her down. Instead they were beckoning, saying, "Come on, girl, get wise," asking that she follow his lead. And she wanted to, as if he were a magnet pulling her toward him. She thought that what they said to each other didn't matter, it was the undercurrent between them that was important.

"After the film we'll cut out," he said. "I want to talk to you." She wasn't at all annoyed that he took for granted she would have no other plans. She knew that she would follow him anyplace that he led her.

"I thought Pat said there was a party," she said.

"Yeah, I guess there is. But we don't have to stay more than a few minutes. It's not really a party, just refreshments here for everyone. Don't worry about it." His smile made her heart do loops. If anyone can stop the bomb, she thought, he can. He's got the face of a hero.

In a short while the Congregational minister asked everyone to be seated, and he spoke a few words to introduce the film. Someone turned out the lights and the room became silent. Jill watched the film, clutching her pocketbook in her lap. She saw mushroom clouds envelop the planet, turning it into an empty wasteland. She watched scientists working on the bomb; soldiers marching to war; and women and children, buildings, farms, and animals get destroyed. She saw demonstrations in different parts of the world crying out against these horrors, and young people like herself and her friends having to leave their schools and homes in terror because of an accident in a nuclear plant.

When the lights came on, there was silence for a few seconds, and then a spontaneous burst of applause. Jill sat quietly; there was so much to take in.

"You okay?" She felt a tap on her shoulder, and looked around to see that Toby was sitting right behind her.

"I guess so. It's pretty strong stuff." She really felt dazed. "It's very powerful."

"I know. That's the point. I'll get you a cup of coffee."

"Thanks. I'll come over with you." She felt the need to get up and walk around, as if to make sure she was alive and in one piece.

"I hope you're not sorry you came," Toby said as they stood with their coffee cups in their hands.

"No, I'm not sorry. Just shook up. It's very scary."

"It's less scary when you're doing something about it." Toby gave her a smile that made her feel she would never be afraid if she were with him.

"What can you do?"

"Plenty." Toby again explained about the demonstration and their need for people to distribute leaflets and to put up posters. "We also need money," he said, "to pay our expenses. Do you think your father would give any?"

"My father?" Jill laughed. "Not a chance. He thinks the plant is fine for the town. Your father does too, doesn't he?"

Toby nodded glumly. "Yeah. He doesn't think much of what I'm doing. But I don't care. I'm doing what I think is right."

"I know. I admire you for it."

"Thank you." Their eyes met. Jill felt as if their bodies were leaning toward each other even though they were both standing still. If they'd been alone, she was sure, he would have kissed her.

"Let's get out of here," Toby said tersely.

Jill saw Pat Foner's eyes follow them as they left the meeting room.

Toby took her to a small Italian restaurant. They sat in a booth and he ordered a pizza for the two of them. "So how did you like the meeting?" he asked.

"It wasn't much of a meeting . . . the film was terrific. There was such a mixture of people. I saw a woman from my father's bank, and an old man named Orlando, who put in some flower beds for my mother once. It wasn't what I expected."

"Orlando's great. He says he wants his grandchildren to be able to live. He's a fantastic worker."

"Do you ever think of anything but nuclear plants and bombs?" Jill met his eyes and studied his face. "I don't even know what to talk to you about," she said with a sudden burst of frankness.

Toby laughed. "What do you want to talk about?"

"I don't know. Everything. Let's start with you. We

live in the same town and go to the same school, but I really know very little about you."

"What do you want to know? I'm just under six feet, I weigh one hundred sixty pounds, when I was ten I fell off a bike and had fourteen stitches across my knee, and my favorite sport is soccer. Now do you know me?" He grinned at her.

"Not at all. You're giving me statistics, not clues. I want to know what you think about when you wake up at four o'clock in the morning. Do you love your mother? Have you any sisters or brothers? I want vital information. What do you dream about? I want things that count." Jill smiled back at him.

"Wow. That takes time, a lot of time. How about you learning about me in small doses? I mean, let's spread it out. Besides it should be an exchange. I should learn about you too. That's only fair."

"Okay, agreed. What do you want to know?"

"How did you live in this town without my knowing you? Where'd you get those eyes from? What are you doing next weekend?" Toby's steady gaze made her feel flustered.

"Next weekend? I don't know, nothing much that I can think of."

"You want to come down to New York with me? I'll show you that I don't really have a one-track mind. There's a fantastic street festival they have in Little Italy. I try to get there every year. Do you like to eat?"

"Sure, I love to eat. Especially Italian food. When are you going?"

"How about going down Saturday morning and spending the day? I'll get my mother's car."

"Sounds super." Jill's voice was calm but her heart was galloping. "You still haven't answered any of my questions."

"I'll take the easy ones first. Yes, I love my mother, most of the time, anyway, and I have a kid brother. That's all you're going to get tonight. Now it's your turn."

"You haven't asked me anything important," Jill said.

"You mean coming to New York with me isn't important?" His tone was teasing but his gray-green eyes were serious.

"I didn't say that. Yes, it's important." Jill realized she was losing her self-consciousness with him. She wanted to be absolutely honest with him. She didn't want to flirt and to play games, because she felt that he would have no use for anything superficial. He wasn't one of those boys who went out with a different girl every week. If he liked someone that was it, and he'd need to know the girl felt the same way. She wanted terribly to be that girl.

Neither one of them spoke much on the way home. Jill kept wondering if he felt as she did, that their brief time together had been important. The emotional impact of the film they had seen together was a bond between them. Frightening as it was, it made her feel that every moment of life was precious. There was no time to waste. She felt sure that he too must be aware of the chemistry between them. The tension she felt could not possibly come from herself alone since with all the boys she had known, she had never felt it before. Of course she had never had this kind of experience before.

If she had any doubts, he swept them away when he kissed her good night. He still didn't say much but simply took her in his arms as if they had known each other forever. The way, she thought, he did everything, without doubts or hesitation.

CHAPTER
FOUR

Jill bided her time in telling her parents she was going to spend Saturday with Toby. She didn't look forward to her father's reaction, and she figured that if she waited until the last minute it would be too late for him to do anything about it.

Besides, she had other things on her mind. The Monday after the film showing, Pat stopped her in the hall to ask if she wanted to help address envelopes that night. "We're doing a mailing giving facts and figures on leaks and accidents in nuclear plants. How documents have been falsified and even federal safety rules, which don't mean much anyway, get circumvented. Can you believe it?"

Jill thought for a few seconds about the book report and math homework she had to do, but she said that she'd be glad to help.

"We're meeting at my house at seven-thirty. Do you know where I live? You turn off Main Street at Bridge, go down two blocks and then into Hop Hill Road. It's the second house on the right, a big old white house."

"I think I know where it is. I'll be there."

She had the sense not to ask if Toby was coming, but her heart raced at the thought that she might see him. She hadn't heard from him since Friday night, but she had only half expected to. She knew he'd had a soccer game on Sunday and probably practice on Saturday. The game was out of town, so she hadn't been able to go to see it.

Never having been in love this way before, Jill was amazed to find how absorbing it was. She wondered what she used to think about before. Now, it seemed that Toby was there behind all her thoughts: when she was sitting in study hall, when she was brushing her hair, when she woke up in the morning, and when she got into bed at night she thought about him.

Monday night Jill asked her mother if she could have her dinner early. "I have to be someplace at seven-thirty," she said.

"Where are you going?"

"To Pat Foner's. She's having a few kids over."

"On a school night?" Mrs. Simon asked mildly. "And who is Pat Foner? I haven't heard you mention her name before."

"A girl at school. I'll be home early." Jill hoped this would be one of the nights her father would be late. He'd ask more questions than her mother. She thanked her good luck that she was just leaving the house when he came home. She gave him a quick kiss and a hurried goodbye and went down the street before he had a chance to say anything.

Jill approached Pat's house a little nervously. She felt like an outsider before she got there. But she needn't have worried. She was given a warm welcome and a place was made for her around the large table where six or seven girls and boys were busy stuffing envelopes. After Jill had joined them, someone suggested they do an assembly-line operation with two people stuffing, two slapping on address labels, and the rest sealing the envelopes. The pile to be done moved quickly that way.

Jill had expected to find a very serious group, but she was pleasantly surprised by the amount of horseplay and joking that went on around the table. One boy, Bill Evans, kept up a running string of wisecracks.

Jill was dying to know if Toby was expected but she didn't want to ask. About three-quarters of an hour after she arrived, he came in. It had started to rain, and his light sweater was drenched and water poured down from his hair and face. Pat ran for a towel and rubbed his head vigorously. Jill watched jealously; she wanted to be the one doing that.

But after a few seconds Toby took the towel from her and dried himself off, then pulled a chair over next to Jill. "How you doing?" He gave her a warm smile.

"Okay." She could feel his nearness and smell the rain-soaked wool of his sweater. Unthinkingly, she touched his arm, and her heart swelled when he caught her hand in a brief, tight squeeze.

It was a little after nine when the envelopes were tied in bundles, ready for the post office. The group broke up to leave and Toby picked up the box of mail to take to his car. "Come on," he said to Jill, "I'll drive you home." But he didn't head toward her house.

"It's a school night, I said I'd be home early," Jill told him.

"I know. But I have to celebrate, and I want to celebrate with you."

"What are we celebrating?"

"I'll tell you when we get there."

"Will you tell me where we're going? You're being so mysterious."

"I thought you'd like a mystery. If you must know, we're going to visit an uncle of mine. Actually a great-uncle, my grandfather's brother. He's a terrific man. You'll like him." Toby glanced at her sideways. "Do you mind?"

"I don't seem to have much choice," Jill said. She was mystified, and felt flattered. He must like her if he was taking her to meet a favorite uncle. But why?

Toby drove to a tiny house on the outskirts of town. The house was made of hand-hewn logs and was set away from the road in the woods. "He's kind of a hermit," Toby explained. "He lives here alone. I guess you'd call him a nature lover; he knows all about the birds and trees and the plants that grow in the woods. He also has a fantastic collection of records; there's always music going, old Benny Goodman songs, jazz, classical—you name it, he's got it."

"He sounds neat, but I still want to know why we're going there." Jill followed him up the path to the house.

"You'll find out in a minute."

Uncle Ben, as Toby introduced him to Jill, was not at all what she had expected. From the few things Toby had said she thought she would be meeting an oddball; but Uncle Ben was a tall, straight, distinguished-looking man, with alert blue eyes and a neatly trimmed white mustache. His rustic house, really a cabin, was comfortable, almost luxurious inside. There were books everywhere, on floor-to-ceiling shelves, piled up on tables, and some even on the floor. There was a fine oriental rug in front of the huge, stone fireplace, paintings on the walls, and large inviting easy chairs. As Toby had predicted, a Brahms concerto was being played on the record player.

Uncle Ben greeted them warmly and offered them hot tea or a choice of soft drinks. Jill accepted the tea while Toby opted for a soda. "I have good news," Toby announced after Ben had served them. "I just got into Yale."

"Good boy," Uncle Ben said enthusiastically. "That calls for a celebration. I'll open a bottle of wine."

"That's terrific." Jill was thrilled that he had wanted to include her when making his announcement.

Ben gave them each a small glass of wine and made a toast. "Here's to another Wells at Yale. I'm sorry it skipped your father, but you can carry on the tradition, my boy." He turned to Jill. "His grandfather and I were both Yale men—I wish he was alive to enjoy this with us."

"I do too," Toby said. "I only hope there's enough money to pay for it," he added glumly. "I lost my weekend job—they're closing down the market where I worked. I've already been told at school that I probably won't get a scholarship. Not because of my marks, but because we're not poor enough. My father had a good laugh when he heard that. I think I can get a student loan for a couple of thousand, and I may get a thousand-dollar scholarship from Dad's company, but there's a long way to go to the thirteen or fourteen thousand you need for Yale. They keep raising the tuition every year."

"Don't forget my promise. You get busy and find yourself another job, and I'll make good my end of the bargain. Whatever you earn I'll double toward your tuition." Uncle Ben gave a hearty laugh. "And I'm not thinking of some measly job either—you earn good money and you'll be pretty well set. Your father can take out a personal loan for the rest. If I had the money I'd pay for it all, but I haven't got it."

"What you're doing is terrific," Toby said. "I hope I can get a good job. There's not a heck of a lot around. Men with families are taking part-time jobs that kids used to get, because of the unemployment. I'll get something, though, you can count on that."

"I am, son."

They sat and talked for a short while, mainly about the

great variety of birds that came to Uncle Ben's feeders. Jill was fascinated by the older man, but she knew she had to get home and she and Toby left before long.

"What does your uncle think of your politics?" Jill asked when they were in the car.

"I think he agrees with me, but we don't talk about it much. I know he was against the war in Vietnam; but he knows my father and I don't agree, and he doesn't want to get in the middle between us. He has a stubborn sense of family loyalty, and he can't stand family quarrels. He is an oddball in his way, but he's a fantastic man."

"I think he's terrific," Jill agreed. "Thank you for taking me there."

"I wanted to," Toby said. When he stopped the car in front of her house, he turned to her. "Jill, I'm not someone who beats around the bush. I'm a pretty serious guy, and when I feel something I take action."

Jill met his eyes nervously. She didn't know what to expect.

Toby smiled. "You look scared. I'm not good at making speeches, and I'm not the romantic type. Heck, all I want to say is that I think you're terrific. I want you and me to be a couple. I don't know who you go out with now, but whoever it is, stop. I want you to be my girl. There's so much for us to do together . . . I feel there are things for me to learn from you and things you can learn from me. I think we'd make a fantastic pair." He didn't touch her, he simply sat and held her eyes looking for her answer.

"That's just the way I feel about you." She was as direct as he was. He touched her face with a gentleness she didn't know he had, and then took her in his arms. She felt as if some miracle had happened that they two, of all the millions of people in the world, had found each other. She held him tight, until reluctantly she said she had to go inside and kissed him good night.

There was a light on in her father's study, and Jill hoped she could get upstairs without his hearing her. Surely the wonder of the last half hour would be written on her face, and her father would ask questions.

But the study door was partly open, and her father called to her. "Jill, you're home pretty late. Where were you?"

She stood in the doorway. Her father was in his big armchair, a lamp beside him and a book in his hands. "Just over at a friend's house."

Mr. Simon smiled. "That's telling me a lot. Where? What friend? Why on a school night?"

"For heaven's sake, Dad, do I have to report everything to you? I'm a big girl now. Not that I have anything to hide. I was at Pat Foner's. She's a girl from school. She had some kids over. Now you know my innermost secrets," she said, mockingly putting her hand over her heart. "Okay?"

Her father was frowning. "I suppose you went with Toby Wells?"

"Suppose I did?"

"I thought I told you I didn't want you to get mixed

up with him." Her father had put his book down on the desk beside him and was clasping his hands in front of him, a gesture Jill recognized as a warning that he was getting angry.

"You don't have to like all my friends. Besides, you never gave me any good reason for not seeing Toby. I happen to like him, and you're not going to stop me from seeing him. He's a very nice and interesting boy. As a matter of fact I met his great-uncle tonight. He's a terrific man. You'd like him."

"I doubt it very much. His great-uncle? You mean Ben Wells? The guy who lives in the woods? He hasn't done a day's work in twenty years. Lives on some kind of government pension he shouldn't be getting—why he was in jail once. You can stay away from him too."

"Why was he in jail? I don't believe it." Jill had been standing in the doorway while they had been talking, but she came into the room now and leaned against her father's desk.

"One of those fool demonstrations like your friend Toby gets into. That was against the war in Vietnam, down in Washington. I think he hit a cop over the head or something stupid like that. They're troublemakers, the two of them. Toby's own father won't have anything much to do with Ben."

Jill couldn't keep from laughing. "Sounds like Uncle Ben. But Dad, that was years ago. You can't still hold that against him. Anyway, it wasn't that he committed a crime. He's a great person."

Mr. Simon looked up at her, his face serious. "Jill, I'm not about to lock you up in your room, I'm not stupid. But I wish you'd take my advice. You'll only get into trouble with these people. They're not going to change anything. You're a young, pretty girl. This is your last summer to just have fun. Next year you'll need a job for college money. What'd you do tonight, stuff envelopes for some dumb mailing?" he asked shrewdly. "Is that your idea of a good time? If you want to occupy yourself with volunteer work, there are plenty of charities. You can work at the hospital a few hours a week if you want to help people. But don't try to run the government or think you kids know anything about nuclear power. Leave it to the people who know what they're doing."

"But they don't know," Jill cried vehemently. "If people didn't speak up we'd be in a worse mess than we are now. The government and industry are killing off our environment and nuclear power can kill us all. I don't agree with you at all."

Her father's face was tense. "You're just mouthing slogans. I'm worried about you, Jill."

"You're not worried; you just want to keep me your little baby girl. You don't want me to think for myself. I'm worried about you, living with your head in the sand. You say work in a hospital, but I want to work so that the hospital won't get blown to bits. I'm going to bed. Good night." Jill went over and kissed her father on his cheek, but she knew that was not the end of her arguments with him.

She went up to her room feeling depressed. The wonderful glow she had felt when she had left Toby was gone, and she was angry with her father for having spoiled it for her.

Jill examined her face in the mirror and was disappointed. She had somehow expected that she would look different, that the deep emotion she felt for Toby would show and have changed her face. She didn't even know how to make her face look troubled. For a few minutes she hated her healthy, rosy cheeks, her smooth, unlined skin, and the clear, dark-blue eyes staring back at her. She didn't at all look like a girl who was going through an emotional crisis, a girl who had fallen deeply in love.

But more than love had happened to her that evening. She had never been a joiner; she had always avoided the clubs in school. Group activities had seemed to her a place for people who didn't know how to do anything by themselves. However, working at Pat's house that night with the others had been an eye-opener. It had been exciting and gave Jill an exhilerating experience she had never thought possible. The sense of camaraderie was part of it, but even more remarkable had been how a somewhat disparate group—kids and a few older people who might have little else in common—had worked together because of what they believed in. For the first time Jill felt that she really understood what Toby meant by people power, the strength of people who got together to fight for a common cause. If it hadn't been for him she might never have known.

CHAPTER
FIVE

When Jill came into the cafeteria for lunch the next day, Pat Foner motioned for her to come over to the table where she was sitting with some of the group who had worked on the mailing. At first Jill felt her shyness return; but they were so friendly and warm to her, she soon felt comfortable.

She was laughing at someone's remark, when her friend Diane came by with Dwight. They waved hello to her, but didn't stop to talk, and Jill watched them with a pang of uneasiness. Diane was her best friend, and she didn't want to lose her. Friendship wasn't something she took lightly.

As soon as she finished eating, she excused herself and went over to Diane and Dwight. "Hi," she said, "can I sit down?"

"Haven't you had your lunch?" Diane asked. Her voice was cool.

"Yes, but I thought I'd come and talk to you. What's

the matter?" she asked Diane directly.

"Nothing. What should be the matter?"

"You're acting peculiar. Isn't she?" she asked Dwight.

"Leave me out of this. But maybe you're the one who's being peculiar."

"What have I done?" Jill asked.

"Okay, I'll tell you." Diane faced her. "You and I have had lunch together every day this whole year. Now all of a sudden you're eating with a whole different crowd without saying a word to me. Wouldn't you think that was peculiar?"

"I guess I didn't think about it. I came in and they asked me to join them and I did. They're a terrific bunch of kids, Diane. They care about what's happening. You should have been there last night. We sent out a fantastic mailing about nuclear accidents. I wish you'd come to one of the meetings." Jill looked from Diane to Dwight. "You too. It's really exciting, Dwight."

"I'll bet," he murmured.

"But it is," Jill insisted. "Don't put down what they're doing, and don't make fun of it. It's important."

"Maybe it is to you," Diane said coolly. "Maybe some of us think it's a waste of time, and that Pat Foner and Toby Wells and their bunch are impressed with their own importance."

"That's not fair," Jill said vehemently. "You don't even know what the facts are, or what they are doing. If you'd read some of the material they have, know the awful things that are happening, how many accidents there have been already in nuclear plants, how dangerous they are, you'd think differently. You could at least have an open mind."

"Boy, they sure sold you fast. Since when have you become such an activist?" Dwight had a smile on his face that she didn't like. "It's a pretty sudden change for you, isn't it? Last week at the Pub you weren't so sure."

Jill was wondering whether to tell him that last week was light-years ago, when Toby came over to their table. He said hello to Diane and Dwight, and then turned to Jill. "Have you got a minute? I'd like to talk to you."

Jill got up. "Yes, I was just leaving anyway. I've got to get to a class in a few minutes. I'll see you later," she said to Diane and Dwight.

She walked away with Toby, but they both heard Dwight say deliberately loudly, "Now I understand her sudden attraction for politics. Very interesting." Jill's face burned, but Toby patted her arm reassuringly.

"Don't pay any attention. Besides, if it's true, I don't care. I'm darn glad to be the one to get you involved. There's nothing wrong with that. You're my girl, aren't you?"

"I guess so." She wasn't yet used to Toby's casual ease in taking charge, although she realized it was that very quality that made him a leader. "What did you want to talk about?"

"About Saturday. We have a date, you know."

"I haven't forgotten." She gave him a warm smile. When their eyes met she felt almost as if they were kissing, as though even a fleeting eye contact bound them together in an embrace. He held her eyes for a few seconds before he spoke.

"We'll be gone the whole day; and tell your parents you'll be home late. I have a lot of things planned. Can you leave early? I'd like to pick you up by eight."

"Sounds terrific. I'll be ready. I can't wait."

"Me either." He leaned over and landed a light kiss on the tip of her nose. "See you."

There was no way Jill could avoid telling her parents that she was going to spend the day with Toby in New York. She waited until Friday night to announce it, and, as she expected, her father was the one to blow up.

"I thought I made myself clear," he said at the dinner table. "I don't want you running around with that boy. I don't like what he's doing and I don't want my daughter mixed up with him."

"But I *do* like what he's doing. I agree with him completely. I've got to think for myself, not just parrot you. You have nothing against him except his ideas. That's like living in some totalitarian country. It's un-American." Jill looked to her mother for support, but Mrs. Simon gave a wave of her hand.

"You should listen to your father," she said. "He knows more about these things than you do."

"I don't know about that." Jill looked at her father defiantly.

"You're already talking like those crazy kids. Calling

me un-American. I can only hope that you will soon see for yourself how foolish they are." Mr. Simon turned back to eating his dinner and Jill was glad to let the subject drop.

Toby was there to pick her up promptly at eight the next morning. When Jill slid into the car beside him, she felt as if she were going off on a wonderful adventure. Toby had the top down on his mother's convertible and Jill let her hair blow in the wind. "This is heaven," she murmured to Toby. She wished they were going somewhere hundreds of miles away so that she could go on riding this way forever, with the sun on her face and sitting so close to Toby she could feel his tan wool sweater against her arm.

Toby was a skillful driver and the drive to the city took less time than she had expected. He put the car into a garage downtown and led Jill to Bleecker Street in Greenwich Village. Jill had only been to New York a few times, and she clung to her pocketbook and to Toby's arm. The variety of people on the streets, Asian, black, European; the noise; the smells coming from the food shops, fresh bread baking, cheeses, sausages and garlic, fresh fish—all made her feel that she had stepped into a foreign country.

"I love it, I just love it," Jill said. Toby's face was beaming with satisfaction.

"I'm glad. I can't stand people who are afraid of New

York. It's a fabulous place, the greatest city in the world. We live only a few hours away, and I know kids who wouldn't come down if you paid them."

Bleecker Street changed as they walked north. The open food stands and the crowded little shops gave way to more elegant antique stores and more expensive-looking restaurants.

Toby found a small Mexican restaurant and suggested they have something to eat. "I thought we were going to eat at the street fair," Jill said.

"We will, but that's later. We have a lot to do first, and the fair gets more exciting after dark."

Jill was content to let Toby plan their day and she followed him into the Mexican restaurant. Toby ordered tacos and enchiladas and glasses of cold fruit punch.

"How come you know so much about everything?" Jill asked him. She felt as though she'd been living in a cave for her sixteen years. He was only eighteen but he was light-years ahead of her.

Toby grinned. "I don't know. I just keep my eyes and ears open, and I like to get around. Sometimes I feel that I don't know anything. When I see all the books in the library, I know I'll never get to read more than a tiny percent of them. And they're only in English. Think of all the things written in other languages, in Italian, French, Russian—I don't even know how many languages there are in the world." He shook his head. "I don't know very much."

"Compared to me you do." Jill looked at him admiringly. "You're being modest."

Toby laughed aloud. "That's the last thing you can accuse me of. I don't believe in people being modest. If you don't know your own worth, who else will? I don't think people should go around bragging about themselves, but don't put yourself down. I have a feeling you do," he added, studying her face.

"Maybe. My parents treat me like such a kid. Like I should just be a child and play with my toys. I don't think my father ever wants me to grow up."

"Fathers have a thing about daughters. He doesn't want to lose you to another man. But he doesn't stand a chance." Toby's eyes met hers, and when he looked at her that way Jill had a surge of emotion that left her feeling weak.

After lunch Toby took her down to Chinatown where they walked around the narrow streets and peered into the shops. Jill was fascinated by the strange foods, whole roasted animals and birds hanging in the windows and the various Chinese delicacies and beautiful vegetables on the streets.

"There's so much to see," she kept saying.

"It would take weeks, months to see all of New York," Toby told her.

Jill expected to be worn out by the time they got to the Italian street fair, but once they were there, she had a second wind. The streets given over to the fair were decorated with festoons of lights, and were crowded with men, women, and children. Music was playing, and there were booths selling everything from food to stuffed animals to religious articles. Toby led her from one booth to another, picking up food for them on the way. They ate sausages, pizzas, Italian ices, pastries, and some things Jill had never tasted before.

It was after ten when Jill said that she thought they ought to leave for home. "Besides, I'm stuffed. I can't eat another thing and I'm not sure I can even walk."

Toby insisted on stopping at one more booth to try to win a doll, but after he'd spent a few dollars and lost, they made their way through the crowds to get to a bus.

When they finally got Toby's car from the garage, Jill sank down on the seat exhausted. "It's been the most fantastic day," she murmured, having trouble keeping her eyes open.

"Come over here and lean against me," Toby said, pulling her toward him. "You can sleep all the way home."

Jill snuggled up close to him and did close her eyes. When she sat up with a start much later, she didn't know where they were.

"You're about three blocks from your house," Toby said, laughing. "You really slept."

"I'm sorry. I guess I was tired."

"I guess you were. Don't be sorry, it was nice. I liked having you sleep against my shoulder. It was good."

When she kissed Toby good night and said goodbye, Jill whispered, "This was the most beautiful day I ever spent in my life."

"The first of many," Toby said, and gave her another drawn-out kiss.

"And you know what," she said sleepily, "you didn't even talk politics." She giggled a little. "I thought you were going to sneak in some political meeting. But it was a day just for us, wasn't it?"

"That's what I wanted. I'm not a weirdo fanatic. My beliefs don't interfere with my love life," he added with a grin.

"I'm glad."

Jill was relieved that her parents didn't wake up when she came into the house. She didn't want anything to mar the joy that she felt. Even another lecture from her father the next day, she decided, couldn't spoil it.

CHAPTER
SIX

Saturday, June first, the day of the protest demonstration, was a moderately warm, spring day. Jill dreaded going downstairs to face her parents because she knew how angry her father was with her. It was with relief that she saw he had left to play tennis when she joined her mother for breakfast.

"It's a heavenly day," she greeted her mother cheerfully.

"Yes, it is." Her mother's face was somber. "Are you really going on that march?" Mrs. Simon asked.

"Yes, I am." Jill poured herself some orange juice and put two slices of bread in the toaster. "I'm sorry you and Dad don't like it. But I have to do what I believe in."

"Your father is very angry. You're upsetting him, Jill."

"I can't help it. I know he's angry, he won't even talk to me. It's not fair. Ouch!" She burned her finger on the hot toaster. "Damn. I'm upset too."

"You always played tennis with him on Saturday

morning. He felt terrible going without you today."

"I'm sorry." Jill's voice was shrill. "I should think you two would be glad I'm doing something important instead of just fooling around."

"You don't need to yell at me. I don't think your father considers what you are doing important." Mrs. Simon brushed bread crumbs from the table into her hand and dropped them onto a plate. Her face was still frowning.

"What about you? What do you think?"

Her mother looked up in surprise. "He knows more about those things than I do. I'm sure he's right."

"Oh, Mother! He doesn't know more because he's a man. You have a mind, you can think for yourself."

"I know that," Mrs. Simon said, and with a slight smile added, "Those new friends of yours are changing you. You never talked like this before."

"Maybe I'm just waking up," Jill said. She ate her breakfast quickly and kissed her mother goodbye. "Wish us luck."

"I wish you weren't going, that's what I wish," her mother said.

When Jill joined the group waiting in front of the old firehouse in the center of town, there wasn't a very large crowd gathered. "It's not nine-thirty yet," Pat said, "and it's called for ten. There'll be a crowd, don't worry." But she looked worried. The local police were out in full force and there were also several state troopers. "They look as if they expect a big crowd," Pat added with a dry laugh.

The crowd did grow, and by the time Pat, Toby, and some others marshaled everyone into lines, many of them carrying posters, there were a few hundred people. Jill had stayed in the background while Toby was busy, but once they fell into line, she walked beside him. "I'm so excited," she whispered to him.

She felt reassured by the crowd, and she wished her father could see them. Her mind searched for the right word to describe the women in their light summer dresses, many with sweaters knotted around their shoulders, and the men in slacks and jackets. *Respectable*, that was it. They weren't people who looked like troublemakers. Young and old, children too, a few babies pushed in strollers—they were all just ordinary people like herself and her parents.

Jill felt a mixture of excitement and pride. While the police hovering around them made her nervous and the stares of the people on the street were uncomfortable, Jill felt that for the first time in her life she had taken a step on her own that had a deep meaning. "People Power NOT Nuclear Power" was emblazoned on one of the posters, and it was that thought that thrilled her. People *did* have power, and she was one of them. She only wished that her father was marching with her, because she could not imagine how, if he was, he wouldn't catch the same sense of closeness to people and of their strength.

The crowd walked down the center of town on Main Street, past the bank where her father worked, past some hecklers who jeered at them, and to the outskirts of town where the construction site was located. Since it takes about eight years to build a nuclear power plant and this one had been started only recently, there wasn't much to see in the way of buildings. There was a tall wire fence around a huge excavated area that looked like a wasteland, the beginnings of some construction already started, a lot of heavy machinery and equipment, and a few men with hard hats working the machines. Apparently a small crew was working overtime on Saturday. "They're sure in a hurry to get this thing built," Jill heard someone say.

The marchers halted in front of the gate to the site. All around them were posts with signs saying "Private Property No Trespassing." Someone stuck an American flag in the ground, and a man whom Jill didn't recognize stood up on a small portable platform Toby produced from a nearby parked car and addressed the crowd. He spoke eloquently of the dangers of accidents and leaks in nuclear plants, concluding, "And who knows when these plants can be turned to make atom bombs and other instruments of war? Do we want this in our backyards?"

The answer came in a loud shout of "No."

When he finished a young woman spoke passionately about the physical danger and psychological effect of constantly living in fear that any moment whole families can be exposed to lethal doses of radiation.

Jill found herself shaken with emotion, wishing that her parents and all her school friends could be there to hear what was being said. However she felt nervous when she saw television cameras focused on them and reporters from local papers taking pictures. What would her father say if her picture appeared in the paper or on the TV news?

The group was getting ready to march back through the town carrying their slogans when the gate opened and a few large trucks approached carrying heavy equipment for the construction. Immediately several of the marchers sprang out of line and lay down in front of the gate behind the No Trespassing signs to stop the trucks.

Horrified, Jill heard a grinding of brakes as the trucks came to a halt. She had closed her eyes in fear, knowing that Toby was one of those who had jumped in front of the trucks. She opened her eyes slowly and was drowned with relief to see the trucks had stopped short of the six figures on the ground: four men and two women, Toby and Pat among them.

But her relief was short-lived.

She heard the police ordering them to get up and out saying they were trespassing on private property, but no one moved. "You'll have to get us out," one of them called.

In minutes the police were half carrying and dragging the struggling six to a paddy wagon. Jill watched frozen until she heard Toby calling her name. She ran over to him. He looked as if he might break in two from the way he was roughly strung between two police officers. "Get hold of my Uncle Ben," Toby yelled. "He hasn't got a phone, you'll have to go out there. Tell him what happened. He'll know what to do. He'll get hold of a lawyer and bond money. Okay?"

He smiled weakly up at her.

"Toby, you okay?" She felt foolish asking.

He grinned. "Sure. I'm fine."

She watched him being dumped unceremoniously into the back of the police van. The crowd cheered, and some of them shouted obscenities as the police car drove away.

The man who had spoken before now shouted through a bullhorn urging the march to continue as planned, pleading for the group to go on peacefully and cautioning against getting into arguments or fights with hecklers. A few people, however, decided to go to the police station to find out what was happening.

Jill looked about for familiar faces, but found she had gotten separated from any of the group she knew. They probably were on their way to the police station to find out about Pat and Toby. She felt helpless and alone, and wasn't even sure she remembered where Toby's Uncle Ben lived. The first thing was to get back into town, and then try to figure out in which direction to go. She knew he didn't live at this end of town. For a few seconds she was tempted to slip away and make believe that she couldn't get hold of Uncle Ben. Maybe she just wasn't the type to be a fighter and without Toby beside her she should just be out of it.

She had mechanically been walking along with the others trying to decide what to do, when an old man walking beside her began to talk. She realized he was speaking to her. "Once they talked about making a park out here," he said. "Right where they're building that plant. A place where kids could play and old people like me could sit in the sun, play chess maybe, meet some friends. Now they make it into a place that can kill people —you call that progress? That's why I'm here. I lived through the Second World War, through Korea, through Vietnam—never has there been a time with no war in all my life. Better to put men to work to make parks, right?"

"Yes, of course. You're absolutely right." Jill turned around to see the man more fully. He was walking with a straight back, but his worn sweater had holes at the elbows, and his face was thin and pale. She wondered if he should be doing so much walking, but she was too shy to say anything. "I wish I could get a hitch back into town," she said to him, ashamed of her fears. "I want to get a lawyer for my friend. He was one of the protestors taken off by the police."

"Maybe one of those trucks would take you," the old man suggested.

He pointed to several trucks that had come out of the construction site. "One of those?" Jill was shocked. "They're the enemy. I couldn't ride in one of those, even if they'd take me."

"Why not?" He gave her a wry smile. "Use them if you need them. Besides the truck drivers aren't the ones to blame."

"I know, but they're working there. They're just thinking of themselves and their jobs."

"They probably have families to support. They're

trapped like everyone else. If you want to get into town in a hurry you can ride with them. Go ahead, see if you can get a hitch."

"Will you come with me?" she asked spontaneously.

The old man shook his head. "No, I march. I have nowhere to go in a hurry."

Hesitatingly Jill stepped out of line and lifted her arm with her thumb pointed toward the village. The second truck that went by stopped. The truck driver looked down at her. "Where you going?"

"Just to the village."

"Hop in." He was a young man, heavily built and with a thick beard. "Tired of walking?"

'Yes, I am." She wasn't going to tell him why she was in a hurry.

"What you doing with that crowd anyway? You don't look the type." He eyed her pleated skirt and lamb's-wool sweater. Pat had advised the girls to wear nice clothes.

Jill laughed. "There isn't any type. There was a wonderful old man walking next to me. He told me not to be shy to ask for a lift. I didn't think one of you would stop. It's very nice that you did."

The young man shrugged. "Don't make no difference to me. You do your thing, I do mine. I work here, that's all. What they're doing ain't no business of mine. I'm glad I got a job."

"Yes, I know." Jill felt that if Toby or Pat were talking to him either of them would explain that it did make a difference and would try to educate the truck driver to their way of thinking. But she didn't feel up to it, she wouldn't know what to say. She knew in her own mind why she was against the nuclear plant, but she didn't know how to put it into words. She couldn't even get her side across to her own parents.

"You can let me out here," Jill said, as they approached a main intersection. "Thanks a million."

"Anytime. Just don't put us out of work, okay?" he called after her, as she stepped down from his high cab.

On the street, Jill tried to get her bearings: she and Toby had started out from Pat's house to go to Uncle Ben's, so they must have come from the road on her right. Did they cross the intersection, or did they turn? If she had only paid attention—but Toby had been so mysterious about where they were going and why, and she had been so intent on him. . . . She studied the four corners; one held a Mobil gas station, one a 7-Eleven store, on the third corner stood a big old brown house converted into apartments, and on the fourth there was a vacant lot. That was it. She remembered going past the vacant lot and thinking that it looked like a dumping ground for beer bottles and cans. Jill hurried past the lot and took the road out of town. She had no idea of how far Uncle Ben's house was, but she was sure that she would recognize it when she saw it.

She walked quickly and every once in a while she broke into a run. The picture of Toby carried between the two policemen never left her mind. His face had been a mixture of anger and helplessness.

Soon she was leaving houses behind, and she wondered nervously how much farther she had to go. And what, she suddenly thought, if Uncle Ben wasn't home once she got there? The thought made her go even faster, thinking, illogically, that if she got there soon enough she would catch him.

When she recognized the wooded road leading to his house, Jill broke into a run, and was breathless when she pounded on his door. She practically fell into his arms when he opened it. His calm face and immaculate appearance filled her with relief, first that he was there and then because his quiet manner was reassuring, as if every day breathless young girls came knocking on his door.

"Come in, come in, it's nice to see you again. I was just about to make myself a cup of tea, can I give you some? Come, sit down. Milk or lemon?"

"I'd love some tea. Nothing in it, thank you. I'm so glad you're here. I was so afraid you wouldn't be." Jill sank into a comfortable chair.

"I'm almost always here. I rarely go out. Here," he handed her a steaming cup.

Jill sipped the tea thirstily. "Toby asked me to come." Quickly she told Uncle Ben what had happened. "He thinks you can get a lawyer and bail money." He was sitting opposite her, and had let her tell her story without interruption. "Can you?"

He spoke slowly when he answered. "I think maybe I can. Sam Powers might be the best lawyer to call. Was Toby going to call his father, do you know?"

Jill shook her head. "I have no idea." She smiled shyly. "I wondered why he came to you instead. I mean. . . ." she stopped, flustered.

Ben Wells smiled. "I guess it's because Toby's father doesn't approve of what he's doing." He leaned toward Jill with a mischievous grin. "I won't come between father and son, but I'm proud of Toby; he's doing the right thing."

"I'm so glad, because I am too. He got me involved and I think he's terrific."

Uncle Ben stood up. "I guess we'd better get going. I don't have a phone so I can't call Powers. I hope he's in his office. He often goes in on a Saturday morning to catch up when the switchboard is off. He doesn't like the telephone any more than I do." Ben chuckled. "Come on, at least I have a car. I don't like modern contraptions, but I had to give in when it came to a car—although many times I wish it was a horse and buggy."

Jill followed him out and into a vintage station wagon; but like Uncle Ben, the car was in immaculate condition, as clean as if it stood in a showroom. Mr. Wells drove carefully and slowly as if the machine might be a horse, not to be overworked. When they got into the center of town, he parked along the green and told Jill to wait in the car while he went up to Mr. Powers's office. In a short while he came back and said that the lawyer would meet them at the police station in a few minutes. He then drove them to the station.

The old red-brick building was familiar to Jill, but she

had never been inside it. She felt self-conscious going up the steps with Mr. Wells, wondering what her father would think if he happened to see her. It was around lunchtime, and with a nervous twinge she realized that he could be going by now on his way home from the tennis court. She ran up a few steps ahead of Uncle Ben.

Inside, the place was crowded with people, and everyone seemed to be talking at once. Jill recognized some of the people who had been on the march. Mrs. Foner, Pat's mother, was there, and the two policemen who had carried Toby away. The six demonstrators were sitting on chairs against the wall looking glum. A police officer stood guard over them. Uncle Ben joined Jill in a few minutes, and they went over to talk to Toby as Mr. Powers came in.

"What do you think will happen?" Toby asked the lawyer.

"What are you charged with?"

"Breach of peace and trespassing on private property. If they try to get me on assaulting a police officer I plead not guilty." Toby's voice was firm but his eyes on the lawyer's face were anxious.

"Did you assault an officer?" Sam Powers asked. He was a short, middle-aged man with a tense, lined face and an amazing pair of dark, intelligent eyes. He spoke in short, clipped sentences.

"I did not. Two of them grabbed me, not very gently either. Carried me to the paddy wagon."

"You couldn't walk?"

"I wouldn't get up." Toby smiled a little sheepishly. "We were all lying on the ground in front of the trucks."

Soon the police officer in command, sitting at a desk on a raised platform, called for quiet. He consulted a piece of paper. "I'll call them up one by one," he said to a sergeant standing beside him. The first name he called was Pat Foner.

"Do you have an attorney or are you representing yourself?" the officer asked her.

"I'm representing myself," Pat said in a low but clear voice. Her mother came up and stood beside her.

"I'm her mother," Mrs. Foner said. "We didn't have time to get a lawyer. I happen to think this is outrageous, pulling these young people in. They didn't do any harm. This is a free country. . . ."

"Please, ma'am, no speeches. Quiet." He banged on his desk to quiet the snickers in the room.

After briefly questioning Pat and then the officers who had dragged her away, the officer in charge said she could go on her own cognizance but to report to the county court at ten o'clock Monday morning for arraignment. Looking shaken but relieved, Pat went to the back of the room with her mother, obviously anxious to hear what would happen to the others. She smiled weakly at Jill, and whispered in passing that since they were all local people she thought the cop would be lenient.

He didn't ask bond money of anyone until he finally came to Toby. Jill thought the officer purposely kept Toby for the last like someone saving the best for dessert.

He didn't waste any time letting his feelings be known. "I know about you," the policeman said. "You're one of the leaders of this thing, aren't you?"

"We are all leaders," Toby said quietly.

"That's what you say," the cop said gruffly. "I've heard about you, seen your name in the paper plenty. Making trouble in school too. Too bad with nice parents like you've got. It says here you're charged with assault on a police officer, breaking the peace, and trespassing on private property. Got anything to say?" He leaned forward on his desk and looked hard at Toby.

"I did not assault a police officer. Actually I was the one who was assaulted."

"Are you making that a formal charge?" The officer's dark eyes glinted.

Mr. Powers stepped up next to Toby. "I'm representing Mr. Wells. We're making no charges here. This is a matter for the court to decide. Can I assume you are releasing him as you did the others?"

"No, you cannot. Two hundred and fifty dollars bond or staying in jail until the court arraignment Monday at ten."

"I'll stay in jail," Toby said curtly.

Mr. Powers shook his head. "No, we'll post the bond. Two hundred and fifty dollars is ridiculous. How about a hundred? My client isn't going anywhere. He'll be in court Monday—I'll be responsible."

"Two hundred and fifty," the policeman repeated sonorously.

Sam Powers gave him an angry glance.

"A weekend in jail might do your client good," the officer said drily.

"Thank you for your solicitousness. Why are you singling my client out? You asked no bond of anyone else."

"Apparently no one else kicked a police officer. Are you paying the bond or do we take your client into the jail?"

"We'll pay the bond," Mr. Powers said curtly. He conferred a few minutes with Toby's uncle and then came back and handed two one-hundred-dollar bills and a fifty-dollar bill to the sergeant standing in attention. Without a word he waited while a receipt was written out and handed to him. Then he motioned for Toby and Uncle Ben to follow him and he strode out of the police station, with Jill behind them.

Jill blinked against the bright sunshine. She'd forgotten what a beautiful, perfect June day it was. Toby took hold of her hand and drew her to him. "Thanks for everything," he said.

"Don't thank me, I didn't do anything. Your uncle's the one."

"You had a long way to go to get him." Toby let out a long, deep sigh. "Thanks to all three of you. What do you think's going to happen?" he asked the lawyer.

"I'm going to find out which judge is on Monday. If it's Litwin we'll be okay. Did you kick anyone?"

"Heck no. I wouldn't have had a chance if I'd wanted to. They were pretty rough, and I struggled. I may have jabbed one of them with my elbow or knee, but it was just to keep myself from getting hurt. I swear I didn't injure anyone."

"You may get a fine. What I don't like is if they say you're guilty and fine you, you'd have a criminal record, and that's something you could do without. It would make you ineligible for a federal job, and wouldn't do you any good in the armed services. That time up in New Hampshire, they didn't book you, did they?"

"No, we were all released. Could I really get a criminal record for this?" Toby looked stunned. "How can they be so crazy? That's the most unfair thing I ever heard of." He shook his head in disbelief. "I didn't do anything. We had a peaceful demonstration. We have a right to do that."

"It's not that simple," Mr. Powers said. "A lot of important people in this town want that plant. It means jobs, it means people coming into town while it's being built. And don't forget it's going to add a bundle of money to the tax list. The police know whom to please. Remember this is a small town. If your father wasn't well known they'd have been a lot tougher. As it is, I think that cop figured he was doing your old man a favor by coming down hard on you. Thinks he's teaching you a lesson."

"Well, he's got another think coming. If anyone thinks this is going to stop me they're crazy."

Ben Wells and Jill had stood by listening to the conversation. Now Jill turned to Toby. "I guess I'd better get going. Is it all right if I come to court on Monday?" She looked uncertainly from Mr. Powers to Toby.

"Of course. I hope everyone comes. I'll need all the support I can get. I'll call you later," Toby said to her.

When Jill got home the house was empty. She was relieved that her parents weren't there, but she felt restless and uneasy. On an impulse she called up Diane. She missed her friend and thought of all the Saturday afternoons they had spent together. It seemed like another world to her, just going shopping or fooling around. Jill waited nervously while the phone rang, hoping Diane would be home but wondering what kind of a reception she would get. She had been so cool recently.

Diane answered the phone. She sounded surprised to hear Jill's voice. "I thought you were on that demonstration today," she said.

"I was. But Toby and Pat and a few others were taken away by the police. Oh, Diane, it was awful, they were carried off like lumps of baggage. The cops were so mean, and they were enjoying it, they really were."

"They were doing what they had to do, I guess. Toby and Pat must have been doing something wrong." Jill felt as though Diane was scolding her.

"They didn't do anything so terrible. They were only trying to stop some trucks from going into the plant site. They weren't hurting anyone."

"But they had no business being there. Honestly, Jill, I don't know why you're mixed up with those kids. They're just not for you. That Toby you're so crazy about likes to make trouble. I wish you'd forget him. You don't belong with him and his crowd."

"You sound like my father," Jill said, walking up and down with the phone in her hand. "And why don't I belong? You think I'm some weakling? It's not just because of Toby. I have a mind of my own whether you think so or not."

"I don't know why you called me," Diane said sulkily.

"I don't either," Jill said, and hung up. When she put down the receiver, she burst into tears.

She felt frightened and isolated, but angry too. It was scary to step out on her own, to have her parents and old friends against her. Yet she also felt proud of what she was doing and resentful that the people closest to her criticized her instead of admiring her for taking a stand on her own.

Ashamed of her crying fit, she dried her tears and decided to go for a walk by herself. She would show them that she was not easily intimidated and that she could get along without them, that is, without Diane, if she had to. "It's her loss," Jill thought to herself, and she went outside into the June sunshine. She headed for a dirt road leading to the countryside and strode along, thinking of Toby and building up an image of herself as what she laughingly thought of as a twentieth-century Joan of Arc.

CHAPTER
SEVEN

Jill had a miserable weekend. Sunday's local paper had a full account of the demonstration and pictures of the six being carried off by the police. They were also on the television news programs. Her father was furious with her and, as she confided to Toby over the phone, treated her as if she had leprosy. She didn't dare meet Toby on Sunday, but instead spent most of the day in her room trying unsuccessfully to read. This must be the way prisoners of war feel, she brooded, isolated in a foreign country.

She hated being alienated from her parents. While they had had their disagreements, she had never before felt separate from them, nor had it ever occurred to her that she could have values different from theirs. She had simply accepted their views, especially her father's, when it came to politics and to people. Now she realized how little thinking she had done for herself, and while she felt she had taken a big step forward, it was hurtful not to have their support.

Somehow or other she managed to get through the long day. She couldn't decide whether to let her parents know that she was skipping school and going to the courthouse on Monday. Jill didn't want to lie to them, but neither did she want to get into an argument with her father. Besides, she feared that he would forbid her to go to court and then she'd have to deliberately disobey him. Jill sat and stared out of her bedroom window. Being a political activist wasn't easy, she thought with a sigh.

As it turned out, at breakfast on Monday she did announce that she was going to the courthouse. She hadn't planned it, but the words just came out. Predictably her father did blow up, but he never said in so many words that he forbade her to go. In no uncertain terms Mr. Simon told Jill what he thought of Toby and his friends, and that it pained him to have his daughter duped by a bunch of "silly radicals," but he ended up rather lamely by saying he could only hope that she would come to her senses and see how foolish she was.

"My colleagues at the bank will have a high old time laughing at me if they hear my daughter's running around with a bunch of reds."

"They are not reds," Jill had said emphatically. She was relieved when he left for work, but hurt that he went out of the house without kissing her or saying goodbye.

Her mother, who had remained silent while her husband had let go his tirade, was, however, visibly upset. "I can't stand these fights with your father," she told Jill when they were alone. Mrs. Simon's tall, thin figure and anxious eyes suddenly looked sad to Jill. For a few moments she felt that she was with a stranger she hardly knew: What went on in her mother's head; what did she think about? Was she a happy woman or was life a big disappointment to her? Did she still love her husband? All these thoughts shot through Jill's mind, and she felt guilty that she wasn't a better daughter, that somehow she should try to get closer to her mother. But it never seemed to be the right time, and besides, she didn't know how. Maybe when she was older, and married herself. . . .

Jill felt uneasy when she arrived at the courthouse. Inside it was crowded with young people whom she didn't know, boys and girls who must have come from nearby towns. After standing by herself for a little while, she spotted a group from her school and went over to join them. At ten o'clock sharp the judge entered the courtroom and everyone stood up. In a few minutes the judge pounded with his gavel and brought the court to order.

The judge followed the same procedure as the police officer, and called each case separately. After the first two, Jill barely listened. She was waiting anxiously for Toby's turn and concentrating on the hope that he would come off as well as the others. So far the judge simply reprimanded each one and let the demonstrator off with a strong warning to keep away from the power plant.

When it was Toby's turn, Jill's heart beat nervously.

He had had a haircut and looked unfamiliarly "establishment" in a suit and tie. She found him particularly endearing, like a kid dressed up for Sunday school.

However, his somber appearance and neat clothes didn't seem to have an effect on the judge. A policeman insisted that Toby had kicked him in the stomach, and Toby's insistence that he hadn't—that perhaps he had accidentally jabbed him while he was being carried— didn't get him far. He was fined two hundred and fifty dollars and Mr. Powers's plea to reduce the amount was denied.

Outside of the courthouse, Jill waited uncertainly for Toby. He was standing on the steps talking with his parents. His father, who had looked grim throughout the proceedings, especially when he had paid the court clerk the fine, still appeared very angry. Mrs. Wells looked more upset than anything. Jill wanted to say something comforting to Toby, but she was too shy to approach the three of them.

But in a few minutes Toby's parents drove away and Jill ran over to him. "At least you didn't have to go to jail," she said. She wanted to throw her arms around him, but there were too many people around. "Was your father very angry?"

"He was furious at *me,* not at *them,* which he should be."

By now Uncle Ben and the lawyer came out of the courthouse and joined the two of them. "That cop was lying," Toby said angrily. "It gets me so mad. I'm not considered a minor, I have to appear in a civil court; but they treat me like a kid. If I'm a kid I should go to the juvenile court."

"You're eighteen," Mr. Powers reminded him.

"I know, but that doesn't make any difference to them. If someone older contradicted a cop they'd listen. Anyway, they're wrong, dead wrong. I didn't kick anyone. I hate being accused of something I didn't do. What really hurts is that my own father wouldn't believe me. But it's not going to stop me, or anyone. Even if I'm on their books I'm going on. Arresting people who demonstrate is only going to make us go out all the more. They'll see."

Jill was fired by his spirit and enthusiasm.

They all stopped to get something to eat, and then Toby and Jill left to go to their afternoon classes.

"Do you really want to go to school?" Toby asked, as they walked toward the high school.

"Not really. What do you have in mind?"

They grinned at each other. "What is so rare as a day in June? I don't feel like going to class. Everyone will be asking a lot of questions. This morning has been enough."

Jill realized he was more upset than he wanted to admit —angry about being treated unfairly and upset by his father's reaction. "Come on, let's go," she said. Toby took her hand and they started to run, but not in the direction of East Compton Senior High.

Toby led her to his house to get his mother's car. "My parents will be away for the rest of the day. Dad had to go to Boston on business and my mother went with him.

They won't be home until late. All I need is for my father to hear I cut school. But I don't care, I need to do something nice after this morning."

"Are you sure you want to?" Jill asked.

"Yes, I'm sure." His eyes convinced her.

Jill had never been inside Toby's house, and she was glad that she liked it. There were lots of books, simple but comfortable furniture, and a pleasant feeling of cozy hominess. He took her down a hall to show her his room, apologizing for its mess. "I was in a hurry this morning," he said smiling sheepishly. He too had a solid wall of books, and a pile of magazines on the floor. Jill had to agree the room was messy, with his clothes strewn about, his bed unmade, and parts of an old bicycle heaped in one corner.

"Don't let the mess bother you," Toby said. He drew her to him, and kissed her long and hard on the mouth. "I told you my parents won't be home until late," he said, meeting her eyes solemnly. "We don't have to go for a ride."

Jill had her arms around his neck, her eyes almost level with his. "I know. I . . . I guess there's one thing you ought to know about me."

"What's that?"

She felt her face was flaming. "I don't know how to tell you. . . ."

Toby laughed. "Are you going to tell me you've got some horrible disease?"

"No, not that. I'm a virgin," she blurted out.

Toby held her tight. "I guess I'm glad," he whispered. When he released her, he was smiling. "I admit it does pose a problem. Should she or shouldn't she?" He put his hands on her shoulders, and stood facing her. "This is something, my darling, you are going to have to decide for yourself. You know where I stand on the matter—I think we have something wonderful going for us—but this has to be your decision, not mine. Don't you agree?" He kept looking at her with his keen, steady eyes.

Jill tried to answer lightly. "And here I was hoping you would sweep me off my feet. I hate making decisions," she answered more soberly, "but I guess you are right."

"Come here," Toby said, and drew her closer. "Let's not make a big thing of it. One of your charms is your innocence, although it beats me how you've managed to come this far being so wide-eyed. You're a rare girl, Jill, and I love you. So come on, let's go for a ride."

It was nice to walk back into the sunshine with Toby's arm around her. But, riding in the car, Jill did wonder what it would have been like if they had made love. The thought gave her a tingling feeling, scary but exciting. Someday she would find out, and she felt sure she would never know anyone she could trust, and love, as a partner more than the boy sitting beside her.

Toby drove out of town and soon turned off the highway onto a country road. "Let's go exploring," he said. "There are some old dirt roads back this way I've never been on."

"I'm game," Jill said. This is what being happy is, she thought: to feel that this minute is precious and that you will have it for always and no one and nothing can ever take it away. She stretched out her hand and touched Toby's arm. He turned to her with a responsive, warm smile, more reassuring than any words of love.

He drove leisurely, picking roads at random to follow. When he'd come to a crossroad he'd stop for a few seconds and then choose a direction. "Do you know where you're going?" Jill asked.

"Of course not. Have no idea."

"We could get lost."

"Yep, we could." He gave her a cheerful smile. "Would you mind?"

"No," she said without hesitation.

After driving up a long hill and coming to a plateau with a stunning view of distant mountains on one side and woods on the other, Toby found a place on the side of the road to park.

"I saw a path through the woods a little farther back," he said, leading Jill by the hand down the road. "Let's see where it goes."

The path was an old wood road, and hand in hand they followed it. Toby seemed lost in thought, and Jill wondered if something was wrong. Finally she asked, "What are you thinking about, or don't you feel like talking?"

"I'm mad at that judge for giving me a record. It burns me up. He didn't fine anyone else."

"I know. It's not fair, but what can you do?"

"I don't know, but it's discouraging. Sometimes I wonder, what's the use? They have all the power, we're never going to get anywhere."

"Oh, Toby, that doesn't sound like you." Jill was shocked by the sudden fading of his exuberance. She had never heard him speak so downbeat before.

"You think I never get discouraged, but I do. Sometimes I wonder if we're wasting our time." He looked at her with a pain on his face she had not seen before. "Don't worry," he added, "I'm not giving up on the creeps."

"I don't ever expect you to give up," she said, and held his hand.

They walked for a few miles and decided to rest on a plot of green moss they found. Jill stretched out with her head in Toby's lap and looked up at the sky through the trees.

"This sure beats school any day," she said, smiling up at Toby. "Are you excited about going to Yale?" She wanted to cheer him up.

"Yeah. I'm looking forward to it, but I'm worried about getting a summer job. There aren't many around."

"You'll get one. With your brains and talent," she added with a laugh. "Say, what's going on? You're the one that usually encourages me. Don't be down. . . ." She pulled his head to her and kissed him. They held each other for a long time. Then Toby stood up.

"This is dangerous," he said looking down at Jill, who was still stretched out on the bed of moss. "I'm not made of iron. You're a very seductive female, you know. I can only hold out for so long, and that time is darn near running out."

Jill brushed some grass from her clothes and stood up. "Okay, I can take a hint." She tucked in her blouse where it had come out of her skirt. "I'll make myself unseductive."

"You'll never do that," Toby said. "Before we go let's leave a mark here. This is our place, maybe we'll want to come back." Taking a scout knife out of his pocket, he looked around to find the right tree. He spied a smooth-barked beech with mostly dead limbs and only a few leaves. "This one's perfect. It's almost gone, so a few scratchings won't hurt it," he said.

Jill watched him etch out a heart and carve their initials on it. She had an amused smile on her face. "I never thought of you as being sentimental," she said when Toby was finished and had turned around to kiss her.

"There's a lot you don't know about me."

"I'm finding that out. But I want to know everything, every little thing," Jill said, and gave him an impulsive hug. It was typical of him, she thought, to make sure he found a dead tree for his carving.

"You may be sorry," Toby replied, holding her in his arms. "You may find out things you don't like."

"Never, never."

As they walked back to the car, Jill was glad to see that Toby had regained his high spirits. They both sang in loud voices, and when they sighted the car, they broke into a run and chased each other to it.

CHAPTER
EIGHT

On the last day of school Jill emptied her locker with
an unexpected sense of anxiety, almost depression.
Ordinarily she and Diane would be talking and giggling
about how to celebrate, and making plans for the summer.
This time she didn't know what the summer would bring.
Toby would be busy job hunting and sooner or later find
something. Dwight hadn't called her since they had gone
to the Pub weeks ago, and she wouldn't go out with him
now anyhow. He knew she was Toby's girl. Pat had
mentioned having to work hard to keep the momentum
going against the plant, but surely that wouldn't take up
every day and evening. . . . Even the thought of being able
to drive didn't seem all that exciting. Where would she
drive to, and besides Jill could only have her mother's car
when she wasn't using it.

She looked around the classroom that already seemed
deserted. The plants that had lined the windowsill had
been taken by her teacher and a couple of students, some-

one had taken the posters off the wall, chairs were perched on top of desks. "Goodbye until September," Jill murmured, and remembered with a further pang that next year Toby wouldn't be there. He'd be in New Haven at Yale. "This is nuts," she said to herself. "I'd better get out of here before I start to cry."

She still felt low when she got home, but her spirits revived quickly when Pat called. "Can you come over tonight?" Pat asked. "A few of us are getting together to plan what we should do next. I hope we can map out a program for the summer."

"Sure. That's great, I'll be there."

Jill spent the rest of the afternoon cleaning up her room and looking over her summer clothes. Most of her things from last year looked tacky and Jill wished she could throw them all away. After much moving of shorts, tops, skirts, and slacks from one pile to another, finally she had a bundle to take to the thrift shop. Reluctantly she put the rest of her clothes back in the closet. Looking around at her now neat room, the accumulation of old school papers thrown in the waste basket, books back on the shelves, and clothes picked up from the floor, Jill felt a great sense of accomplishment.

When she heard her mother come in she called her to come upstairs to see what she had done. Mrs. Simon was properly admiring. "It'll be nice to have you home for the summer," her mother said a bit wistfully. "In another year when you go to college I feel that you'll be gone. And I'm glad you'll be away from that crowd at school

—the ones who do all that demonstrating. Your father's been very upset about you."

Jill's heart fell. "But I won't be away from them," she said gently. "I'm not going to lie to you and Dad. I intend to work with them this summer. And you may as well know that Toby Wells is my boyfriend. Dad's not going to stop me from seeing him," she added quickly. "I'm sorry he feels the way he does."

Mrs. Simon's lined face looked more worried than usual. "He's going to be very angry. I wish I could make you change your mind."

"You can't. I'm sorry." Jill looked at her mother's anxious face. "You keep quoting Dad. What about you? Can't you understand how I feel? Once you were in love with Dad, weren't you? You never talk about when you were young."

"It seems so long ago." Her mother sighed. "Yes, I was in love." She gave Jill a smile. "To tell you the truth my parents weren't too happy about it either—my coming east to marry your father. But it wasn't because they disapproved of him. They didn't like our living so far away. This is different."

"But you don't know Toby. Neither one of you do. He's a fantastic person. I wish you'd give him a chance. If you'd let me invite him over for supper one night you'd see for yourself."

Mrs. Simon looked shocked at the thought. "Your father would have a fit. I don't think you'd better do that."

"For heaven's sake, Mom, he's not a monster," Jill said

crossly. "Anyway, I'm going to be seeing Toby, okay?"

"It's not okay, but what can I do?"

As often with her mother the conversation drifted off, left hanging in midair. Mrs. Simon never seemed to be definite about anything except her garden. Jill wondered that she ever had been able to decide to leave home and come east with Jill's father. She made up her mind that she was going to level with her father that night. She wasn't looking forward to it, but she felt that she might as well get it over with. She didn't want an argument every time she went out with Toby or did something for the protest movement.

Jill got out of her school clothes, took a shower, and got ready to go to Pat's house later. Her heart beat nervously when she heard her father come in, but with a last look at herself in the mirror for reassurance, she went downstairs. Mr. Simon had brought home two new shirts that he had bought for himself, and Jill hailed this as a sign that he was in a good mood.

"Let's see them," she said, after kissing him hello.

"They're just ordinary shirts, nothing to look at. Where are you going? You look dolled up." He took a can of beer out of the refrigerator and sat down at the kitchen table. Mrs. Simon was busy at the stove, and Jill was setting the table.

"No place special." Then, steeling herself, Jill plunged in. "As a matter of fact, I'm going over to Pat Foner's. We're planning our program for the summer. As I told Mom I intend to work with the group, and you may as well know I intend to see a lot of Toby too."

Mr. Simon put down the catalog he had been glancing at and surveyed his daughter. He stared at her for a few minutes without speaking. "What is this, a declaration of war?" he asked, his face impassive.

"I hope not. I don't want to fight. That's why I wanted to tell you so there wouldn't be a hassle every time I went out with him." She saw her father try to hide an amused smile. "That makes sense, doesn't it?" she asked more lightly.

"From your point of view, I suppose. As I said before," he said in a resigned voice, "I'm not about to lock you up in your room, and I think you're being extremely foolish." He shrugged. "If you want to waste your time in this way I don't suppose I can stop you; it's your time and your life. I'm disappointed that you should have so little sense."

"That's your opinion. I hope history doesn't prove that we're right about the nuclear plant. That we don't have another Three Mile Island accident—that's all I can say."

"That's enough. Your dramatics doesn't carry much conviction. It's not going to keep me awake nights."

"Okay, keep your head in the sand." She turned to her mother. "How soon do we eat?"

"In a few minutes."

Her father put down the catalog he had picked up again, and slammed his fist on the table. "What you're doing, you're doing, but we're not having our meals timed to suit your idiotic meetings, just get that through your head. We'll eat when dinner is ready and we'll take our time doing it."

"Yes, sir," Jill said meekly.

At Pat's house Jill found the usual crowd from school with the addition of some older townspeople. She joined the group sitting around a large table in the Foner family room. Pat's mother hovered around serving coffee and cookies. Jill felt a pang of jealousy that Mrs. Foner was working with her daughter, and that in fact she turned out to be one of the more outspoken objectors to the nuclear plant. She was a small, plump woman whose conventional house and neat, undistinguished style gave no hint of her passionate convictions when she opened her mouth to speak. She looked like a woman who could be devoting her life to cooking for her family, but instead she turned red with anger when she talked about the nuclear plant.

Jill had sat down next to Toby; and with her sensitivity to his moods, she knew immediately he was down again. She waited for a break in the discussion to ask him why.

"I thought I had a job but it fell through," he said. "I don't have a darn lead on another."

"You'll get one, I'm sure you will," Jill said.

"I wish I could feel as optimistic," he said glumly.

"If you don't, you can work on this all summer. This is important." She looked at him, wishing they were alone so she could kiss the unhappy look off his face.

"Oh, great. And not go to college. A lot of good that

94

would do. Outside of everything else my father would kill me. Uncle Ben would feel terrible too. I haven't absolutely decided but I've almost made up my mind I want to go in for medicine. That's pretty important, don't you think? I'd like to do research, not just practice."

"I think it's wonderful. You'll get a job, I know you will. I feel it in my bones."

He reached for her hand under the table and held it.

A lot of people spoke and many ideas were tossed around and discarded. Jill listened to it all, at the same time conscious of Toby beside her and her hand in his. She felt shy about speaking, and when Pat turned to her at one point and said, "You haven't said anything, Jill. What do you think?" Jill flushed and said she would go along with whatever the others decided.

A general program for the summer was finally adopted —they agreed to prepare and hand out leaflets every weekend at supermarkets and shopping malls, to conduct a discussion group regularly, and to prepare for another large demonstration around the middle of August. "We'll also have to do some fund raising to pay for everything," Toby said. "Run some parties or bake sales or something. We should set up a fund-raising committee right now."

"Good. You be the chairman," Pat said.

Toby groaned. "I might have known. Should have kept my mouth shut. I'll do it if Jill, Mrs. Foner, and Hugh," he nodded to a boy Jill knew slightly from school, "will be on the committee." They all agreed and when the meeting broke up, the four of them got together and arranged to meet the following Friday night to plan what to do.

As Jill left with Toby, she felt highly elated. "It's going to be a terrific summer," she said. "I was feeling low earlier, worrying about what I was going to do, but now I'm excited. Aren't you?"

"I'd feel better if I had a job, or if I knew where to find one. Every place I go I hear there are practically no summer jobs for students this year. Too many people out of work, and men with families are taking any job they can get. I don't blame them, but it's tough on someone like me."

"It's only the beginning of the summer." Jill looked at him pleadingly. "Don't get discouraged so fast. You can't have looked very much yet."

"But I have. I've been looking for at least a month, maybe more. Way before school was over. I wanted to get something lined up. I was sure I'd get something too. Now I'm not so sure, and I don't know what I'll do."

They were walking toward Jill's house. It was a bright starlit evening, a half-moon lighting up the sky, and Jill didn't feel like going home. "Let's do something," she said. "Maybe I can cheer you up." She hated to see Toby this way. His black mood frightened her. It was like the one he had had the day of his trial. He had seemed like a stranger then, and she had felt that he was slipping away from her.

"What do you want to do? I haven't any money."

"I have a little. But we don't have to spend any. We

could go for a walk; it's a gorgeous night. Let's walk around the pond," she cried enthusiastically. "Remember, that was the first place we ever went to together."

Toby's eyes brightened. "Okay, let's go."

It didn't take them long to get to the path around the water, but there under the shadow of the trees it was much darker and Jill clung to Toby's arm. They walked in step with each other, talked about the meeting, about plans for the summer; and when Toby stopped suddenly to take her in his arms and kiss her, Jill felt she had never loved him so much as at that moment. It was as if her love had taken on a new dimension because she had been able to lead him out of a depression. "We're so lucky," she said, her arms clasped around him. "That of all the millions of people in the world we should have met each other. I feel so good with you."

"Will you always feel that way?" Toby tilted her face so that he could look into her eyes. "Would you love me no matter what I did?"

"I can't imagine your doing anything that would make me stop loving you," she said. He kissed her again as if he needed to confirm a solemn promise by putting a seal on her words.

When they walked home and Toby left her at her door Jill thought about her earlier gloom. How wonderful life is, she mused, to go from one extreme to another in less than a day. And again the thought echoed in her mind, how lucky we are!

CHAPTER
NINE

Jill found the days slipping by effortlessly. When she wasn't busy working with the committee, she would help her mother with her planting and then stretch out on the grass, looking up at the sky and thinking about herself and Toby. Being in love, she decided, could take up a lot of time. She could lie that way for hours, not bored, not restless, hardly aware of time ticking away.

There were times when she did miss Diane, mainly because she wanted so much to have someone to talk to about Toby. After the last miserable phone conversation she had had with Diane, when they had both hung up, she had thought it over and called her again. After all they were old friends, and Jill felt sad that their friendship could come to an end because they disagreed about an issue. Friends should be able to disagree, Toby had said, and Jill had decided that he was right. But the second call had been another failure. Diane had said that yes, of course they could still be friends; but when Jill suggested a date, Diane had been evasive. Finally she had blurted out that she was going with Dwight now and she thought it just as well that she and Jill didn't see each other for a while.

"But I don't care that you're dating Dwight," Jill had said. "I was never in love with him, and I have Toby. I don't understand. . . ."

"Well maybe it bothers me," Diane had said. "It's nothing I can explain. But you've changed. We have different interests now. I'd want to talk about Dwight and I'd feel funny discussing him with you. I just think we'd better let things ride for a while. Maybe in the fall when we're back in school it will be easier—I have no hard feelings, honestly. I hope you have a terrific summer. . . ."

Jill had hung up close to tears. Later when she told Toby he had made fun of Diane. "I don't know what you think you're missing. You're better than she is. You have lots of friends, you don't need her."

Jill hadn't pursued it further, although she knew that she would never feel close to Pat Foner or other girls in the group the way she had with Diane. She used to be able to talk to Diane about everything, however silly, but with Pat everything was serious. Jill couldn't imagine just sitting around with Pat and giggling the way she and Diane used to do.

Yet after a while she thought about her friend less and less. She was very involved with the antinuclear group, and she felt that her life had reached a kind of calm plateau, in spite of her father's continued disapproval.

They had arrived at an uneasy truce with Jill not talking about what she was doing and her father venting his anger mildly, with occasional deprecating remarks about the whole group. On these occasions Jill didn't argue with him, but instead concentrated on thinking about Toby. She also bolstered her confidence by thinking that she was doing something right and important.

To raise money for leaflets and for advertising the August demonstration, the group planned to run three nights of old movies in July at the Congregational Church. Jill had volunteered to arrange to get the films, and she had asked Toby to go over the catalog with her to see what was available and what they could afford to rent.

"I don't think you should come to my house," she told him on the phone. "It will only get my father excited."

"Then you come here."

"Is that going to be all right? I mean, your parents aren't exactly enthusiastic either."

There was a brief silence at his end. "My parents won't be home. They're away for the weekend. Anyway, they wouldn't mind. I have something to tell you when you come over."

"What? You have a job? Is that it? Don't keep me in suspense. . . ."

"I'll tell you when I see you," he said firmly. "Come over around seven-thirty, okay?" Then he added in a softer voice. "We'll have the house to ourselves. We can celebrate."

When Jill hung up the phone she felt flustered. Maybe what he had to tell her didn't have to do with a job at all. His voice had sounded so . . . so seductive. The word itself made her blush. It was only ten o'clock in the morning when they spoke, and Jill knew she'd be waiting all day for seven-thirty to arrive. It was the last week in June and they wanted to show the films around the middle of July, so Jill decided to spend part of the day making up a schedule of dates and planning how to publicize the series.

She sat at her desk with a legal-size yellow pad and a calendar in front of her and tried to keep her mind on what she had to do. But her thoughts kept wandering back to Toby.

Although his kisses were always passionate and his touch made her aware of both her innocence and her desires, he had kept to his word and not been demanding sexually. Yet her own yearning made her sometimes wish he would not wait for her decision. What if he took matters into his own hands? But Toby wouldn't do that. He'd say that was chauvinistic. "A girl wants sex just as much as a guy," he told her once. "I don't want any girl to do something just to please me, or to use sex to go out with me. She has to want it and be honest about it, and know what her feelings are about me. I want a girl to be open with me."

Jill had thought a lot about what he'd said. She didn't want to do anything just to please him, but when she did hold him off she felt old-fashioned and coy. She hated feeling coy. She wanted to be open and honest with him, and unafraid. She couldn't deny that she thought about going to bed with him. She thought about it a lot. Then why didn't she do it?

Jill felt nervous the whole day. She went outdoors and lay in the sun, more aware of her body than ever before. She looked at her long, tan legs—she had a good body, strong but feminine. She tried to imagine Toby's face if he could see her naked. Would he think she was beautiful? Had he been with many girls? Would she seem childish and awkward to him? She kept thinking of his voice when he'd said, "We'll have the house to ourselves. . . ." It had been full of what? Promise? Hope? Had he been telling her this was the perfect time for her to make a decision. With a shiver she realized that was exactly what she was telling herself.

When her mother came out to the garden, Jill put a pair of shorts over her bikini and went to ask if she could help. She wanted to feel close to the earth, to quiet her fears. After all, wasn't sex the most natural thing in the world, a part of nature, the very core of its existence?

"Hi, Mom, what can I do?"

Her mother was squatting on the ground, and she looked up from under the wide brim of her hat. "Oh, do you want to help? How nice. You can put some of the impatiens in the rock garden. Anyplace you see an empty spot. Aren't they a heavenly color?" Mrs. Simons sat back on her heels to admire the persimmon-colored plants. Jill gathered up the small, fragile plants and walked over to the rock garden. She went back to get a trowel from her mother and then, crossing her legs under her, sat down on the ground to work. It was peaceful to sit in the sun, to sift the brown earth through her hands and gently pat the delicate plants into place. Idly she watched two young cardinals fight over a few sunflower seeds that had fallen on the ground from the bird feeder. Jill laughed at how angry they were with each other one minute and then flying away together the next.

Gradually her uneasiness subsided. She would let what happened happen. Her love for Toby filled her with a new sense of repose, a feeling that she was growing into a woman, one to match his manhood. There was nothing to be afraid of. She was not a terrified kid, but a young woman who could be open, express her emotions, make a decision. The world looked good to her, working with her mother in the sunlight of a June afternoon, when suddenly she thought of the excavating and the work going on only a few miles from their house. Jill shivered in the warm sun: if the nuclear plant was built, one accident could wipe them all out, or at best force them to leave their homes. And if the plant should turn to making bombs, or if there were a war . . . the thought shattered her beautiful contentment. She looked at the young plants in her hands and thought of their destruction. Jill put them into the earth quickly, but the peacefulness she had felt was gone. She wanted to stand up and yell to the sky, "Stop! Stop, stop!" She did stand and look up at the sky, thinking if there is a God up there He would make them stop. He will not let them destroy this planet.

"I'm going for a walk," she said to her mother.

"Have a nice time," Mrs. Simon said, lost in her own work or thoughts.

Jill headed for an old wood path in the woods, trying to regain her sense of peacefulness. She wanted to feel close to nature, because she believed that somehow it had a force of its own which would endure and make the earth survive. If God produced trees and flowers, sky and sunlight, and singing birds, why would He produce a race of men who would destroy all of it? Jill walked the path, stopping to pick a small bouquet of violets. Her sudden surge of panic and terror had made her think of the evening ahead, and she realized the two were not unconnected. With the world so precarious, why wait for anything? She might not live to love anyone else but Toby.

Toby had left the door unlocked for her, and Jill found him sitting at a workbench in the basement, planing a piece of wood. The large basement room was unfinished but it had a comfortable, homey look. There was a Ping-Pong table in a corner, a rather dilapidated old studio bed against a wall, a few chairs, and an outdoor trestle table with matching benches.

"What are you making?" Jill asked after Toby stood up and kissed her.

"A stand for my records. My old one's stuffed full."

"Don't buy so many," Jill told him. "What's your news?"

She walked around the room nervously, aware of Toby's rolled-up sleeves and his strong arms, aware of the bed in the room. Aware of him—his smell and presence, his strong sexuality as he hammered a last nail into place before pushing his tools aside to face her. Jill stood close to him and silently willed him to know what was in her mind.

The room, the surroundings, nothing was as she had imagined her first real love-making to be. She had never thought of a particular place, but in her fantasies there had been soft lights, perhaps a summer's breeze coming through an open window, music in the background. She smiled because it didn't matter. Toby was there, and that was all she cared about.

Tentatively she put her hands on his shoulders and watched a questioning look pass over his face; and then gently he put her hands down and led her over to sit against the bolsters on the bed. She looked up at him warily, and then down at her hands, twisting a ring she wore on her left hand. She had not thought to tell him in so many words that she had made her decision. She had believed that he would know by just looking at her.

"I have something to tell you," he said.

Suddenly she was frightened. Was he going to break off with her? Was he in love with someone else? No, it couldn't be that; he had said they were going to celebrate. Then she realized that he was nervous too. For the first time since she had known him, he was actually nervous.

"Well, tell me."

"I have a job, and I'm going to make quite a bit of money, but I'm not sure you're going to like it. But you've got to understand. . . ."

"For heaven's sake, what are you going to do? Smuggle dope, peddle cocaine?" Jill looked for release in being silly. "You're making me crazy."

Toby took a deep breath and looked directly at her, then turned his eyes away. "I wish it was something that exciting. I'll probably be digging ditches." He looked back at her again. "Okay. I'm going to work for the construction company on the power plant. Listen," he went on hurriedly, as Jill's eyes widened and stared at him uncomprehendingly. "There isn't another job in town, and it's practically July. I've only got two months to make some money. My dad knew the foreman and got me the job. He said if he was willing to borrow money to send me to college, I couldn't afford to turn down a job, especially one that pays so well. I don't know what he'd do if I didn't take it. Scholarship is definitely out, the thousand dollars from his company is iffy, and I can't get a loan for more than two thousand. You don't know my father. You heard my Uncle Ben say he didn't go to Yale. That was because he couldn't afford it. He went to some crummy two-year junior college instead, and got his engineering degree later. My going to Yale means a lot to him.

"I told him that even if I earned fifteen hundred dollars by the end of the summer it would be a lot. But that means three thousand from Ben, and with the loan, he'll still have to borrow around five or six thousand. He'll do it, but he hates being in debt and he hates having to pay interest. I don't have much choice."

Jill kept staring at him. She moved away from the arm he had around her, and just looked at him. "I can't believe it," she finally said. "I can't believe it. There's always a choice, you've told me that. You've said that people have to make up their own minds, not let others decide for them. I respected you when you said you wouldn't make a decision for me, that I had to decide myself."

"That's completely different," Toby said. "You were making a decision about your body. You had to decide that."

Jill stood up, facing him. For a minute she wanted to laugh. He was playing a terrible unfunny joke on her. Then the irony of the situation penetrated. It *was* funny —terribly, horribly funny. Suddenly she thought of her father, how he would laugh if he found out about Toby's job. How Diane and Dwight would laugh. Diane would giggle until she cried if she knew the whole truth, that Jill had perfumed herself and put on the silk chemise her grandmother had sent her from California, which she had never thought she'd wear, to come to Toby's house that night. That she had decided she loved him so much she wanted to make love. That she had thought about it all day. That she *had* made a decision.

"Don't look at me that way," Toby said. "I'm not committing a crime. It's only for eight weeks. It's not going to change how I feel. I'm still me, I still believe the plant is rotten."

She just kept looking at him with an unblinking stare until he came over and shook her. "I've got a job," he yelled. "Aren't you glad I got a job? It's not going to make any difference whether I dig ditches or someone else does. It's not going to change anything."

"It makes a difference to me," Jill finally spoke. "I can't believe you're serious. I thought you were the most terrific person I'd ever met. I thought you had high ideals, that you were so fantastic. I was in love with you. God, what an ass I am. Everything my parents said was right —you're nothing. You're a phony. I wish I'd never met you. I'm so ashamed. . . ." She turned away, the tears running down her cheeks. "My father said I was a sucker, and boy was he right. Was he ever right," she said between her sobs.

She groped for her bag and walked toward the stairway. Toby grabbed her and held her back. "Listen, you've got it all wrong. I know what you're saying, and what you feel. But you're not a sucker, you're not. I'm the same person. I need the money and there's the job. Working there isn't going to make any difference one way or another. It's not going to change anything about stopping the plant. Going to college is important, and spending two months digging for that stupid plant isn't going to cut any ice one way or another." He was still holding her. "My father would kill me if I didn't take it."

"Let go. I want to get out of here. You don't know anything, you just don't know." She had a wild impulse to hit him, and did, banging her fists against his chest.

"You don't know anything about feelings, about people. You're a lot of talk, a lot of hot air. That's what you are, a big, inflated balloon."

He let her pound him. "Go ahead, get it out of your system. I never saw you so passionate. I didn't know you had it in you."

"No, you didn't. You didn't know anything, and you'll never know. If you did you'd laugh. It's very funny. You don't know how funny it is."

He took hold of her wrists and pulled her to him. "If I knew what?"

She looked up into his face. "You will never know," she yelled at him. "Never, never. Let go."

He smelled her perfume and he caught her eyes. "You've never worn perfume before."

"I've never done a lot of things before," she said. She could see on his face that the truth was dawning on him. She pulled herself free of him, clasped her bag to her chest, and ran up the stairs. She was out of the door before he could catch her, and running down the street.

After a few blocks, exhausted and out of breath, Jill slowed down to get her bearings. She had run, not caring where she fled. She realized she had gone in a direction opposite from her house, but it didn't matter. She didn't want to go home anyway. She kept walking, too distraught and wound up to do anything else. She could hardly believe it was still the same day, that only that morning she had been in the garden, lying in the sun, thinking of Toby. Of Toby and love. She clenched her fists with frustration and anger. She should have hit him harder. Never could she ever forgive him, never.

As she walked through unfamiliar dark streets, her only wish was that she need never see him again. She fervently hoped she would not run into him over the summer, and that when he went away to college in the fall he would disappear from East Compton. Furthermore, she decided, she was finished with Pat Foner and that group. If Toby could turn around and do something like this, she could no longer trust any of them. She couldn't bear to see them, let alone work with them.

Jill felt humiliated. Her own tremendous enthusiasm, her wonderful sense of well-being in believing that she had found a purpose and a remarkable love at the same time, now came back to mock her. Even as she walked she muttered to herself, "What a fool I was, what a stupid, ridiculous fool. And to think I was ready to make love with him." She winced thinking about it.

She didn't know how long she walked, and the thought of having to cover as much ground to get home suddenly frightened her. She felt so tired. She had walked even farther than she had realized and it seemed hours before she was near home. She had to pass Toby's house on the way, and she ran past it as if the devil might come out to catch her.

When Jill approached her house, she slowed down. The thought of facing her parents stopped her. She remembered again the warnings her father had given her about being taken in, about how he had predicted that sooner or later she would be disappointed in Toby. She would never, never in a million years admit to him that he had been right. Jill didn't know what she would say to her father if and when he found out she wasn't seeing Toby anymore, but she vowed that she would never reveal the real reason to him.

Thinking about her parents made her feel more isolated and alone. Because she could never tell them what happened or let them know how hurt and betrayed she felt, the wall between them would be more of a barrier than ever.

When Jill came into the house her mother told her that Toby had called. "He sounded agitated," Mrs. Simon said. "He said for you to call him no matter how late it was."

Jill glanced at the clock, surprised that it was only ten. She felt as if it had to be at least midnight. "Did you have a fight with him?" her mother asked.

This question coming from her mother took Jill by surprise. Toby must have really sounded disturbed to have made such an impression on her.

"A good thing if she did," her father remarked from the chair where he was reading.

Jill bit her lip to keep from crying again. Suddenly she decided that she couldn't bear to have any future discussion about Toby in the house. She didn't want to be questioned and she didn't want her parents to mention his name.

"If it's any satisfaction to you," she said fiercely, looking from her mother to her father, "I'm not seeing Toby anymore. It is something completely personal between us and has nothing to do with anything else." Her lie gave her the courage to add, "And I don't want to discuss him anymore. Good night."

As she turned away toward the stairs, she saw the look of astonishment on her father's face turn to an amused and pleased smile. She spun around. "And don't you say, 'I told you so,' " she yelled. "You told me nothing, nothing at all."

"Did I say anything?" Mr. Simon asked mildly, still with a smile on his face. "But you can't blame me for feeling relieved that you've come to your senses."

Jill ran up the steps to her room and slammed the door behind her. Once inside she flung herself on her bed and burst into tears, muffling her sobbing with a pillow against her face. For a few moments she allowed herself to wallow in a surge of hate: for her father, for Toby, for the whole antinuclear group; and with a fresh flood of tears came a sharp, knifelike stab of pain and pity for herself, for the loss of her love and her trust. To her mother's knock on the door, asking if she was all right, Jill managed to call out a somewhat shaky, "I'm okay. I'm fine," and only cried some more.

CHAPTER TEN

As far as Jill was concerned the days that followed her breakup with Toby passed in a twilight limbo. She got up in the morning, or, as she put it to herself, she got out of bed, which was different. She lounged around the house in her bathrobe dreading the long hours ahead of her. She watched some television; she put nail polish on her toes and fingers, or took it off to change the color; occasionally she went shopping with her mother; she walked to the library to exchange books; and in the afternoons she sat in the sun and read.

Even her mother, usually myopic about her daughter's activities, gave her concerned looks. "What about Diane?" Mrs. Simon asked after a week or so of this behavior.

"What about her?" Jill asked, feigning innocence.

"Why don't you see her? You two were such good friends."

They were sitting on the terrace. Mrs. Simon had fixed

Jill's favorite lunch, and to please her mother, she had eaten half of the fried egg and onion sandwich. "We were friends, we're not anymore. People don't stay friends forever."

"That's an odd thing to say. Some people have the same friends for a lifetime." Her mother sipped from the glass of iced tea she held in her hands.

"Maybe I'm like you. I don't need any friends." Jill stretched out her legs in front of her to examine her suntan. She had on a scant bikini, planning to take a sunbath after lunch.

"Don't be like me," Mrs. Simon said quietly. "I'm not a good example of anything."

Jill looked up in quick surprise and was moved by the expression of sadness that hovered on her mother's face. The look passed swiftly and Mrs. Simon smiled, as if in apology for revealing herself. "I'm not good at making friends, and it's not a good way to be. I don't recommend it."

It was true, her mother didn't have any close friends. She knew a lot of people and with her husband did some entertaining and went out with other couples in town, but they were mostly people Mr. Simon knew in business. Unlike other women Jill knew, her mother didn't have any really close woman friend.

"Maybe I am like you though. Maybe I don't need a best friend," Jill said.

Her mother shook her head. "I think you do. Why don't you call Diane? You're mooning about that boy, and that's foolish. I'm sure whatever happened between you and Diane wasn't very serious. Call her up and ask her to come over," Mrs. Simon coaxed.

Jill was surprised that she welcomed her mother's concern. She had been feeling so hurt and vulnerable, she was grateful to have someone show care and attention; she wanted to be loved and protected. She didn't expect any miracle to happen, yet she felt that if she and her mother did become closer, the summer might not turn out to be a total disaster.

As for Diane, Jill herself had been wondering if she dared call her. She wanted to, but she was afraid. She didn't want to talk to Diane about Toby yet she knew that if she saw her, she'd probably pour it all out. Toby had called several times but Jill had told her mother always to tell him she was out. She had sent Pat Foner a note saying that something had come up and she couldn't work with the group that summer. Pat, she was sure, would surmise that the "something" had been Toby, but she couldn't worry about what Pat thought. Jill wondered if Toby was still working with them, although she didn't see how he could be. She tried not to think about Toby, yet not a day passed that he wasn't in her mind.

During the second week of her misery, Jill awoke from a fitful night of bad dreams and made a decision: she had to do something to pull herself out of the morass in which she was sunk. And in a flash she knew what it was. Jill got out of bed with more energy than she'd had since the breakup. She got into jeans and a shirt quickly and downstairs asked her mother if she could borrow her car.

"Yes, I guess so, but have it back by noon, please. I have to go out. Where are you going?"

"I have some errands to do," Jill said evasively. "I'll be back on time."

She ate her breakfast hurriedly, kissed her mother goodbye, and left. Mrs. Simon's eyes followed her out of the door; she was obviously pleased that her daughter was at least going someplace. If she only knew, Jill thought.

Jill loved to drive and as she pulled out of the driveway she wished she had the whole day to spend by herself in the car. It was warm and muggy, with an oppressive heat that could end in a thunderstorm before night. She had rolled down all the windows, but the air in the car was still uncomfortably hot. Yet the heavy day suited Jill's mood. She was carrying a burdensome load that she planned to get rid of once and for all.

Jill headed for the country, hoping desperately that she could find the place again. She drove up and down dirt roads, backtracking if they didn't seem the right ones, trying to keep calm but knowing she was obsessed. Her goal was to wipe Toby out of her mind. The thought had hit her that morning—she had to find the tree that he had marked with a heart and their initials and scratch it out. In the kitchen she had taken a small, sharp vegetable knife and slipped it into her pocket when her mother wasn't looking. While she was driving she felt in her pocket every once in a while to reassure herself that it was there.

If anyone had asked her to explain why this was going to exorcise Toby, she could not have said. Yet the very physical act of driving the car, of finding the right road to that path in the woods was already a release. She felt somewhat mad riding around the woods by herself. Every once in a while she turned on the radio loud to feel connected with the outside world, and then she'd turn it off to become immersed in the quiet sounds of the forest.

If only she had paid more attention when Toby had been driving. She kept looking for a familiar sign, teasing herself with the memory of how much in love she had been that day. When she spied a parking place by the side of the road, her heart jumped nervously. This was it, this was where they had parked the car. There were ruts still left in the road where the car had been. Jill pulled into the same tracks and stopped the car. When she got out she noticed that the sky had darkened, and the path in the woods looked forbidding. But she wasn't going to turn back now.

She ran along the path, stumbling and almost falling a few times, glad that she'd had the sense to wear her sneakers instead of her clogs. But would she be able to find that tree? Or even the place where they had sat on the ground?

Had they gone this far? She couldn't remember for how long they had walked, but it seemed to her they hadn't gone so far. The sky was getting darker and Jill was terrified of being caught in the woods in an electric storm. But she kept on going. She was discouraged, wondering if she should turn back and come on a better day, when she saw something small and pink in the grass. She bent down and picked up a shiny button. Her button. It had come off the shirt she had been wearing that day. Later she had looked all over her room for it, not knowing where or when she had lost it. Jill felt triumphant. This was an omen. They had been sitting there, and to the left was where Toby had walked and marked the tree. She ran over to the dying beech and yes, there it was: the heart with their initials clearly etched out. Jill took out her knife and slashed at the tree. She drew the knife savagely across the heart, crisscrossing cuts every which way, frightened by her own fierceness. There and there and there. So much for Toby Wells. So much for his high ideals. So much for his superior knowledge, so much for his leading her on, and for his attractive smile and his arrogant body. So much for making her fall in love with him. For wanting him.

When she was finished, the carving was wiped out. Jill glared at the tree with satisfaction. When she ran back to the path, she could hear thunder in the distance. She ran as fast as she could, fleeing the growing darkness, the approaching thunder, the sudden flashes of lightning. The rain began while she was still in the woods. A cloudburst of water drenched her in seconds.

When she reached the car she got inside without shaking off her soaked clothes or hair, not caring that she sat in a wet puddle.

Jill sat for a few moments, her heart thumping, before she turned on the ignition key. She felt relieved because she had reached the safety of the car, but her earlier excitement was lost. She was really no better off than she had been before: she had lost Toby and she had lost the inspiring sense of purpose that he had so briefly given her. Yet her morning's activity had done something for her. For two weeks, even as she had known she was finished with Toby, her mind had been trying to find a rationale for what he had done. She had gone over a hundred times everything he had said to her that night—his parents' pressure, his desperate need of money, the promise he had had from Uncle Ben, the tremendous advantage of going to Yale—trying to find a way to excuse him and be convinced by his reasons. But now she knew that was over with. She could never forgive him. She was finished with Toby Wells *and* his ideas.

That afternoon, while her mother was out, Jill got up her courage to telephone Diane. It wasn't easy. She went over to the phone a dozen times and then walked away from it, to roam around the house and the garden before coming back to where it hung on the kitchen wall. When she finally dialed Diane's number and listened to the ringing, she half hoped there would be no answer. But after a few rings, Diane's voice was at the other end.

Her old friend was clearly surprised when she recognized Jill's voice, but she recovered herself quickly. "Hey, how have you been? Are you still on this planet? I haven't seen you anywhere."

"I'm still around," Jill said, trying to sound as casual as Diane. "I was wondering how you've been."

"I'm good. What have you been doing?"

"Nothing much. Just hanging around."

"I suppose you're busy with that antinuclear bunch. I saw a poster about another demonstration." Diane said it good-naturedly, although Jill wondered if she was mocking her.

"As a matter of fact I'm not working with them anymore." Jill waited for Diane to say something, hoping she wasn't going to ask a lot of questions. There was a dead silence for a few seconds. Then all Diane said was "Oh."

"What are you doing this afternoon?" Jill asked to fill in the silence.

"Nothing much. Is it still raining?"

"No, it stopped. I think the sun's trying to come out. You want to come over?"

"Sure. Now?"

"Why not. Bring your bathing suit. If the sun comes out we can sit outside. Maybe get a swim in our neighbor's pool."

"Okay."

Jill was genuinely glad to see Diane. Having her there again was like coming home after a distant journey. She sensed that Diane felt the same way. After eyeing each other curiously to see if there were any changes, they had both laughed a little self-consciously. "You'd think we hadn't seen each other for years," Diane had said, "the way we're examining each other."

"I know," Jill agreed, laughing with her. "I haven't turned gray and neither have you. As a matter of fact your hair got a lot of red in it from the sun. It looks terrific."

It was easy sailing after that. The sun had come out, and the two girls went outside to sit and talk.

Jill eventually got up her courage to ask Diane if she was still seeing Dwight Armstrong. "Yeah, we still see each other. But we've been talking about going out with other people. I want to, but Dwight doesn't. But I think I will anyway."

"Won't he get mad?"

"That's his problem." Diane turned over from her back to her stomach. "What about you? Do you still see Toby?"

"No, that's over with. Finished." Jill became engrossed in rubbing suntan lotion on her legs.

Diane gave her a curious glance, but all she said was, "Was it that bad?"

Jill laughed. "No, but it was an experience. Someday I'll tell you about it."

"That's all right," Diane said. Later when the girls went indoors to get something to drink, her friend said, "I'm glad you called me. I missed you."

"Me too. I'm glad I called, and I'm glad you're glad." They both giggled.

"We're all glad," Diane said.

It didn't take long for Jill to slip back into her usual summer routine—sitting around with Diane, playing tennis, going swimming, watching television, and going to the movies and to parties. She didn't go out on any dates, but found herself being paired off with Teddy Atkins a lot of the time. Teddy was a broad-shouldered boy who jogged to keep from getting fat, and never went with any one girl for too long. He played the drums and wrote some songs that Jill thought were pretty good. She liked Teddy but he was not someone she would ever fall in love with. "Probably," she told Diane, "because he isn't that interested. I think he likes to have a girl around because it's the thing to do, but he doesn't much care who she is."

"I'm not so sure," Diane said. "I think he likes you."

"Yeah, I know, the same way I like him. But there's no emotion. I know."

"You mean not the way you were in love with Toby."

Jill frowned. "I'll probably never be in love with anyone the way I was with him. You know what they say about first love." She shook her head with an impatient gesture. "I wish I could forget about him. I thought I had, but I haven't. It's stupid."

"You still don't want to talk about it?" The girls had been playing tennis and were sitting at the side of the court having a cold soda.

"I can't. I made a fool of myself and I'm ashamed. Maybe someday, but not yet."

"Well, if you won't, you won't." Jill could see that Diane was annoyed.

"Please don't get mad at me. I haven't talked about it to anyone. It's all too dumb." Jill was close to tears.

"Okay." Her friend was immediately sympathetic. "Anytime you're ready, I'm available."

"I'll remember that," Jill said gratefully.

CHAPTER
ELEVEN

The town was plastered with posters. As the time drew closer to August fifteenth, the date of the demonstration, it seemed to Jill that everywhere she looked there was another reminder of the protest movement. She felt plagued by them. Also there was the mail. Apparently her name had gotten on some mailing lists, and the Simons' post-office box was swamped with literature about nuclear dangers and with solicitations from all kinds of liberal magazines and organizations.

"I wonder why you're getting all this junk mail," her mother said, handing a batch of envelopes to Jill.

"I don't know." Jill looked at the contents briefly, but she felt a twinge of conscience when she dropped them into the wastebasket. She thought of the people who had taken the time to prepare the material, had probably spent hours going over mailing lists, and had worked hard to raise the money for what they were doing. Deliberately, however, she put them out of her mind. She wasn't going to be taken in by any more do-gooders; she'd learned her lesson.

It was a Saturday morning and her father had his car out of the garage and in the driveway, waiting for her to go to the tennis courts with him. He had persuaded her to go back to their old routine. Jill had picked up her racket to join him when her mother handed her another letter. The envelope was the kind one bought in the post office, and could have been a business letter except for the large, scrawled, handwritten name and address. There was no return name but Jill knew immediately it was from Toby.

Her father was honking his horn impatiently, and Jill folded the slim letter and put it into the pocket of her white shorts. She wanted to be alone to read it.

On the tennis court, Jill couldn't keep her mind on the game. After she double-faulted on her serve for the third time, her father became exasperated. "You're not paying attention," he said. "If you don't want to play, say so."

"I guess I don't," Jill said meekly. "I'm sorry."

Her father only got more annoyed. "You could have told me. I would have gotten a game with someone else. You know how I look forward to my Saturday-morning game."

"I said I was sorry. I didn't know I didn't feel like playing until I got here. But I'll play, it's your serve."

Mr. Simon walked back to his service line with a scowl on his face, muttering about the self-involvement of teenagers.

It was a relief to Jill when the game was over. She hadn't given her father a good game and she knew he was still annoyed with her. On the way home he stopped at the hardware store to pick up some fertilizer for her mother, and to try and make peace Jill went into the store with him. Once she had gone inside, she wished she hadn't. Toby's Uncle Ben was making a purchase, and when he saw them he came over and greeted Jill warmly. Her father stood by with a cold look on his face.

"Hear you and my nephew don't see each other anymore. Sorry about that." Ben Wells stood facing her as if he wanted to say more. Jill introduced him to her father. Uncle Ben put out his hand, and Mr. Simon shook it reluctantly. She wished her father wasn't there so that she could talk to the old man alone.

"Toby's a good lad," Uncle Ben said, his bright eyes looking directly into hers. "He's still young, remember that. Maybe what happened between you two will be only temporary. I was glad to see him going with a nice, smart girl like you." His voice boomed out unembarrassed, as if he was unaware of Mr. Simon glaring at him.

"Thank you," Jill said, sensing that he was trying to tell her something. Her father took her arm and was heading her to the back of the store. "Goodbye," she called to Toby's uncle as she saw him leave, wondering what he might have said to her if they had been alone. She could hardly wait to get home to read her letter.

Mr. Simon didn't say anything and neither did she. He bought what he wanted and drove them home. Yet seeing

Uncle Ben made her think of Toby in a less harsh way. Maybe she hadn't been fair with him, maybe his parents had pushed him harder than she realized to take the job. Although Uncle Ben hadn't said anything and probably only guessed why she wasn't seeing his nephew anymore, he made her feel guilty that she had been too quick and too sharp with Toby. What Toby had told her that night had come as such a blow, and she had been so full of what she had imagined the evening was going to be, perhaps she had never given him a chance. He had no way of knowing that that was the night she had decided to say yes to him.

When Jill got home she ran up to her room, closed the door, and took Toby's letter out of her pocket. She looked at his handwriting a few seconds before opening the envelope. The letter was clear and brief:

Dearest Jill, I have to see you. Please do me this one favor. I will not bother you again if you don't want me to. This is very important to me, and I don't think half an hour of your time is asking too much.

I'll be at Holbrook's Monday at five. I'll wait for you.
Toby

She read the letter over several times before she folded it and put it back in her pocket. Holbrook's was an ice-cream place outside of town on the highway. She and Toby had gone there together a few times. Jill didn't much like the place. When it had opened she had expected it to be an old-fashioned ice-cream parlor with little glass tables and wrought-iron chairs. But it was nothing like that. It was rather bare with harsh fluorescent lighting, a long counter where the ice cream was served, and a few benches along the wall. There was no private place to sit down. Jill wondered why Toby chose to meet at Holbrook's, except that not too many kids they knew went there. Usually it was filled with tourists getting off the highway.

There was no question in her mind about going to meet him. Jill knew she would even before she'd read the letter, and she knew before she'd opened the envelope that that was what he would ask her. You don't love someone the way she had loved Toby and then put him out of your mind, or, she thought moodily, lose your connection with him. It was strange to feel so joined to someone whom you hated at the same time. From the very first day she had talked to him, standing in the cold in front of the school the day he went to Washington, she had known he had a hold over her. When they had started going together the ropes had tightened around her more and more.

You can't loosen them so easily, she thought, and even when you do, the bruises leave deep, sore marks. She would go to meet him. She owed him that.

Jill walked into Holbrook's at exactly five minutes past five on Monday. Toby was standing near the door waiting for her. Her first thought was, how good-looking he is. His skin was darkened to a deep tan and his gray-green eyes by contrast glowed in his face. They were like the headlights of an approaching car. He was wearing his work clothes, and he exuded the healthy strength and vitality of a man who worked outdoors. She hadn't been prepared for the way her heart turned over, just looking at him. He had never been more appealing.

He smiled when he saw her, a relieved smile, and she had the feeling he had been waiting there long before five.

"You don't want to stay here, do you?" Toby asked. Nothing about being glad she had come. He knew she would.

"No, I don't. I wondered why you'd picked this."

"I don't know. It seemed kind of neutral," he said with a wry grin. "A place where you could leave your car and we could go from." He took her arm. "Come on."

She didn't ask where they were going, and he drove away from the village. He took her to a place she had never been to before. It was a rustic-looking place off the highway with a bar and a small dining room. It had a cozy, intimate feeling. She wondered if he came here with a new girlfriend.

She felt foolishly relieved when he said, "Some guys at work told me about it."

They sat in a booth. He got a soda for each of them and then sat across the table, just looking at her. "I've missed you," he said after a while. "I miss you a lot." He leaned across the table, touched her hand, and then sat back. "It's been hell. I think about you all the time. Even my parents are worried." He gave a small grin. "I don't seem to be able to sit still."

She sat and listened, looking at him, sipping her soda, but staying quiet.

"I'm ready to give up the job. It's not worth it with you feeling the way you do. Will you give me another chance?"

She looked at him steadily. "Another chance at what?"

"At going together again. What else?"

"You mean you'll give up the job because of me?"

Toby nodded, but he didn't speak for a long time. Jill watched his face, realizing that he wanted to choose his words carefully. "I've been doing a lot of thinking," he said, "and yes, it is because of you, but a lot of it has to do with me too. I really care about you, and I think I did something terrible. I never thought you were going to drop out of the whole movement because of me. That really got me." He gave her a sheepish glance. "I didn't realize I had that much influence."

Jill flushed. "I was turned off. You did do something terrible."

"I'm not talking about the job, I'll get to that in a minute. I mean what I did to you. It was like opening a door and then slamming it in your face. I'm sorry I let you down. I'm the one who got you involved and then because of me you dropped everything. I feel responsible."

"Is that why you want to quit the job now? I don't want *that* responsibility. You'd be making me responsible for what you do now." She looked at him defiantly.

Toby shook his head impatiently. "Don't confuse things. I'm not asking you to be responsible for me. I want to quit the job because I love you, and I hurt you by taking it, and I don't want to do that. I can't make it any plainer."

"What about all your reasons for taking it? What about college, your parents, your father?"

"I don't know. I have no ready answers. I'll have to deal with all that. Maybe I won't go to Yale. Maybe I'll go to a less expensive state university. I don't know. My father will be furious, I'm sure of that, but," he added, with a wry grin, "I can handle that better than losing you." He leaned across the table to her, and his eyes were solemn. "That night at my house, when I told you about the job. You had made a decision, hadn't you?" His eyes were searching her face.

She didn't answer his question. "Don't you think you should figure your future out before you make another switch?"

"I didn't make a switch," he said, with a note of desperation. "I didn't change my ideas, you did."

"I can't buy that. You can't tell me you can go to work in a place that you don't want to see get built. That doesn't make sense. Really, Toby, I'm not a fool. You are helping to build it, every hour you work there—you are helping it to exist."

He gave a weary sigh. "Okay. But its existence doesn't depend on my job—has nothing to do with it. My feelings about the plant didn't change. Can't you understand that?" He was almost yelling.

"Don't shout. I can hear you," Jill said.

"Okay, okay, I'm sorry. But darling, not everything's that simple. There are contradictions. Nothing is absolutely pure. You had an idealistic image of me. It was a darn flattering one, but I'm just a guy. Come down to earth. I'm not perfect, I don't even want to be. I'm a fighter and a realist. You have to be. I made a choice. I decided two months of work was a means to an end and that the end was worth it. Maybe you would have chosen differently. Now I've decided it wasn't worth it, because I was losing you and that tipped the scale the other way. Can't you understand?"

"I don't know if I can," she said. "I just don't know."

They sat silently staring at each other for a while. "I still feel that you're putting the burden of your decision on me." She shook her head. "I don't want to take that on. I don't want to feel guilty if you don't go to Yale."

"I'm not asking you to. Forget about the job. Forget everything else. Do you love me?"

Jill sat with her elbows on the table, her head resting between her hands. "I don't know. Honestly, I don't know. I can't answer that."

Toby's lips tightened. His eyes were darker indoors than out in the sun. "I guess that's that," he said glumly.

Jill groped for the right words to tell him how she felt. He was still the most attractive boy she had ever known, but he had come down to earth for her. It had been her fault to think he was so fantastic, to have endowed him with so much. But he was stumbling like all the other kids she knew. Suddenly, with a cold shock, Jill felt what she and Toby, what they were all facing, what they all had to deal with. When did kids ever before have to grow up with the fear of a nuclear war hanging over them? "Maybe you thought you were doing the right thing," she said, "and maybe I expected too much of you. That wasn't your fault. But now your wanting to quit because of me . . . well, it makes me uncomfortable. Either you believe in what you do, or you don't. And your actions have to fit your words. I don't know that I go along with a means to an end."

"You've never had to make this kind of decision," he said fiercely. "You don't know what you would have done. I don't believe in *any* means to an end. I don't believe in terrorism. I felt I was making a small compromise."

"I know you did. But maybe it seemed big to me." Jill spoke in a low voice. "I guess I'm disappointed. I built you up too much. You came on pretty strong." She gave him a weak smile.

"You don't know me at all," he said savagely. "You had me down as some nerd without any emotions. I don't know what you thought I was—a robot working for a cause? You treat feelings like they're something that don't count. You think only girls and women have emotions that get in the way of how they think, or what they want to do? That a man whose feelings get mixed up with his ideals is weak? Maybe I am weak; so what? Christ, I don't know what you expect of a guy. I'm only eighteen." He stood up. "Come on, let's get out of here."

He hardly looked at her when he got the check and paid it. She followed behind him to the car.

He drove her back to the ice-cream parlor quickly and silently. When they got to her car, he leaned across her and opened the door. "Hope you have better luck next time finding your hero," he said.

"Thanks, thanks a lot." Jill got out of the car as angry as he was.

She drove home with tears burning her eyes, and ran up to her room without stopping to say hello to her parents. She was angry and hurt. Furious with herself for caring about Toby and thinking that being honest with him was going to change anything. But, even worse, he somehow had managed to make her feel in the wrong, that she was being rigid and judgmental. She banged around her room in frustration. She kicked clothes and books lying on the floor, and punched pillows on her bed. Her anger was stifling her, but she didn't know what to do with it.

Finally, although it was almost time for supper, she put on her running pants and shoes and went downstairs. "I'm going out," she called, and ran outside before her mother could tell her it was time to eat. She ran steadily until the physical exertion quieted her down.

When she came home she felt at least more relaxed. She was resigned to the fact that she had to forget Toby once and for all because there was nothing she could do to change the situation. She prayed that she could stop thinking about whether he was right or wrong, or if she was. It didn't matter anymore. "Get that through your thick head," she told herself, "and don't forget it."

CHAPTER
TWELVE

To forget about Toby wasn't all that easy. A few days after her meeting with him, Jill told Diane she had seen him and that he wanted to get together again.

"So, why not?" Diane asked.

"I don't know. I'm really mixed up." Jill had never told Diane why she had broken off with Toby, except to say that he had done something she didn't like. Even now, though she wanted to talk about him to her friend, she had a sense of loyalty that kept her from telling Diane that he had disappointed her. She felt also that the way she had set Toby up on a pedestal was a reflection on herself. She was foolish to have been so impressed and to follow him so blindly.

"But you thought he was so terrific," Diane said. "What turned you off?" They had been swimming and were lying in the sun to dry off.

"I wish I really was turned off. I still think about him. Maybe I expected too much of him. He was involved and he got me involved—but now, well, like I told you, he did something I didn't like."

Diane laughed. "I knew you were involved with that antinuclear crowd because of him. I never thought you cared that much about things like that."

Jill didn't answer, but she felt hurt. Her feeling came as a great surprise to her. Unknowingly, Diane had said something that made her feel cheap.

Jill spent the rest of the afternoon with Diane but she didn't mention Toby again, although he was much on her mind.

She was still thinking about him, and about herself, that evening. After turning off the television because she wasn't really watching it, she went upstairs to her room. Diane's words had cut deep: had Toby really been the only reason she had wanted to work against the nuclear plant?

She knew very well that without him she might never have gotten involved; but she thought about all the things she had learned, the facts about the dangers and the buildup of nuclear arms. That hadn't been just Toby talking. She had been convinced herself.

Jill studied her face in her mirror. She saw a healthy girl with clear skin and eyes, and a somewhat sad, wistful expression on her face. Jill tried to look at herself as a stranger would. What kind of a person is that?

"I'm worse than Toby," she said to her reflection. "I blamed him for blowing hot and cold, for working for the plant because it suited him—but I started because of him, and then I dropped out because I was hurt. What kind of a jerk am I?"

Her face flushed with remorse and a terrible sense of shame. *Everything my father thought, that Diane thinks —it's all true.* The thought mortified her: she didn't want to be a silly teenager. It wasn't fair to blame Toby for her actions. That was what she had accused him of doing. When they had been talking she had felt that he had let her down, and was still letting her down. That too was unfair. Jill wondered if it was possible to be idealistic in a real world, and if it was even wise to be. But one had to have standards and values. Toby had once said you had to keep working at something until you won. Who was it that said you could lose a battle but win the war? Maybe that was it. Toby's taking the job and her deciding to stop working were just setbacks, battles along the way.

When Jill went to bed that night, she didn't fall asleep for a long time. She kept going over in her mind the complexities: the age-old question of preserving your integrity in a world that was not black and white, not a simple good and evil, but many shades in between. No ready, easy answer came to her because, she figured out, there were no blueprints or fast rules. A person had to deal with each situation as it happened. She remembered that she had hardly thought twice about taking a ride in one of the trucks that was being used to build the nuclear plant. Because Toby needed her and there was no other way to get back to town quickly, that had been an easy, spontaneous decision. Toby's had been a much more important and difficult one to make. Who was she to sit in judgment on him?

Before finally falling asleep, she resolved to decide for herself whether to go back to work with the antinuclear group or not. This time, it must have *nothing to do with Toby.*

The next morning Jill searched her desk futilely, knowing that she had probably thrown out all the literature she had gotten from the group. She also knew that she really didn't have to read it again. She knew what the pamphlets said.

The date was August thirteenth. The demonstration was two days away. Everyone would be at the headquarters and there would be a lot of activity. Jill didn't see how she could possibly have the courage to walk in and face the group. They probably wouldn't even want her around anymore.

"I have some shopping to do this morning," her mother told her at breakfast. "You want to come with me?"

"I don't think so. I think I'll stay home. If I go out, I'll leave a note."

Jill sat across the table from her mother and thought, How strange. I am probably making one of the most important decisions of my life, and my mother doesn't know a thing about it. She couldn't imagine even discussing her problem with her. Mrs. Simon would nod her head and say, "Do what you think best, dear."

Studying her mother's composed face with the faraway

look in her eyes confirmed what Jill had already decided. She didn't want to be removed. She wanted to be involved with life, and she wanted to live. She wanted to make choices and to act on what she believed in.

She waited until her mother had gone and scribbled a note saying she might not be home until late in the afternoon. Then she left the house. Jill knew exactly where the headquarters was, but she took a circuitous route to get there. She was very nervous about facing Pat Foner's cool, efficient eyes. She expected her to say, "Thank you, but we have all the help we need," and Jill could hardly blame her. Then what would she do?

It was worse than going to the dentist, she thought, or heading for an exam. There was no way she could walk by the storefront headquarters without being seen, so once she turned into that block she had to go through with it.

As Jill had expected, the small, bare store the antinuke group had rented was filled with people. Some were using a small battery of phones at one table, others were folding leaflets and stuffing envelopes, some were just standing around talking. Jill immediately felt the same sense of excitement that had caught her in the beginning. She had hardly said hello to Pat when a girl with pigtails thrust a box into her hands and said, "The date on these got blurred so we've been going over them by hand. Can you do this box?"

Jill gave Pat a bewildered look. Pat laughed. "See, we've missed you. You came just in time. Come, you can

140

sit over here." Pat pushed a pile of pamphlets out of the way and made room for Jill at a table with the pigtailed girl and a few women and men. They were all busy working, and with a nod and a smile at Jill, went on with what they were doing.

Jill felt as if she had never left. She had to laugh at her earlier nervousness, realizing that it didn't matter to anyone why she came or why she had left. Another pair of hands was sufficient to make her welcome.

In a short while she felt completely comfortable, as if she had come back to a place where she belonged. Now she even liked the anonymity of being with people who knew very little about her and cared even less. They were all there together to do a job and were bound by a cause they felt deeply about—their private lives, their troubles, and their joys were irrelevant. Nowhere, Jill realized, had she felt such a warm sense of camaraderie. Even thinking about Toby was less painful. For the time being, at least, he had fallen into second place in her thoughts.

The hours flew by. With the others she took a break and had a sandwich and a cup of coffee. The girl with the pigtails, a plump girl with a plain face and the confident air of a pretty girl, kept Jill amused with detailed accounts of the movies she went to see apparently every night of the week.

When Jill left it was almost six o'clock. She couldn't believe the day had flown by so fast, in great contrast to the way the hours had dragged for her the rest of the summer. On the way home she made up her mind to tell her parents where she had been and what she was doing. No one could accuse her now of doing something because of someone else. She had acted strictly on her own belief, and that gave her a sense of independence she had never known before. Jill felt almost free of the hold Toby had had on her. A part of her might always love him, and she had to be grateful to him for having introduced her to a world of ideas and to the responsibility of taking sides. But now she was on her own, not dependent on him for an incentive. While she still hated that he was working for the nuclear plant, she could no longer hate him for doing it. It seemed a peculiar division, but that was the way she felt.

Both her parents were home when she got there. The day had cooled off, and her father asked if she wanted to play some tennis before dinner. Jill's first impulse was to say no. It had been a long day and she was tired; but her father had already put on his tennis clothes, and she realized he had been waiting for her.

"Sure, I'll change my clothes."

When they got to the tennis court Mr. Simon said, "I hope you can concentrate on the game this time."

"I think I can," Jill said. She knew that she could as part of her new-found freedom: there were some choices she didn't have to make. She didn't have to draw a line between working with the antinuclear group and doing a lot of the things she had always done. She wasn't a fanatic and didn't want to be a lopsided person. She could be serious about demonstrating against a nuclear buildup, and at the same time enjoy herself the way she always had. In fact the very joy of living was the best reason to save it. Jill slammed a service ace across the net and laughed gleefully when her father's racket couldn't touch it.

When they got home, Jill took a shower and put on a pair of clean white slacks. Then, after joining her parents on the deck while her father had his before-dinner beer, she made her announcement. "I went back to working with the antinuclear group," she said. "In case you hadn't noticed that I'd quit for a while."

"We noticed," Mr. Simon said. "You going with that Wells boy again?"

"No. He has nothing to do with it."

"I'm glad of that," her mother said.

"You hardly knew him," Jill said impatiently.

"I knew about him," Mrs. Simon said. "Your father knew enough about him."

As always Jill was irritated by her mother's dependence on her husband, but she kept her mouth shut. "Anyway, I'm not going with him," she said.

"That's good at least," her father said tartly. "I'm sorry you haven't some sense about that plant. You know how I feel about it and about the people who are against it. A pack of ignoramuses."

"That's what *you* think, but I don't agree with you. And you can't say I'm doing anything hasty. I've thought about it a lot, and I want to do everything I can to stop the buildup of all nuclear power. This new plant is just part of it."

Mr. Simon shrugged. "I think it's a stupid waste of time. We need nuclear energy and we need a defense as strong as our enemies'. But you're welcome to your opinion. I can't stop you." He gave a wry smile. "I may not agree with you but you have a right to believe what you want. That's what makes a democracy."

Jill, who had expected a big fight, felt somewhat disappointed, as if she had wanted to try out her new sense of independence and wasn't being given a chance.

"I'm glad you feel that way," she mumbled, suspicious that her father was still treating her indulgently, like a child. That's his problem, she thought. I know that I have changed, that I have grown, so I don't care what he thinks. He'll probably treat me like a kid even when I'm married and have kids of my own. The thought was oddly comforting: Some part of me will always want me to be the kid and him to be the father. She pictured her father as a strong guidepost that she could hold on to or move away from, but who would always be a constant figure in her life. She never thought of her mother that way. Mrs. Simon was too removed, too vague, a person who lived alongside her but whose existence, whose thoughts, were not deeply entwined with her own. No matter how much Jill might disagree with her father, his impact on her was there. The big thing, she thought, was not to be afraid to disagree.

When they sat down to dinner, Jill felt that she had made a great leap that day.

* * *

August fifteenth was a hot, muggy day. Jill's first thought when she got out of bed was that it mustn't rain. She immediately imagined a small, wet, and bedraggled crowd and her heart sank. That would be awful.

She dressed quickly and gulped down a cup of coffee and a donut for breakfast. "Today's your big day," her father remarked over his more leisurely bacon and eggs. "Just don't get arrested."

"I won't, don't worry. Not unless they arrest all of us."

"You mean all six of you?" her father asked with a grin.

"There'll be a big crowd, don't worry." Jill wished she was as confident as she sounded.

"That's the last thing I'd worry about," Mr. Simon said. "Have a good time. You're not going to change anything, so you may as well enjoy yourself."

"Don't be so sure we won't," Jill said sharply. "Your life may be saved whether you like it or not."

Her father looked at her appraisingly and affectionately. "I'd hate to depend on that crowd to save my life."

"No, you'd rather depend on the Pentagon to kill it." She gave her father a defiant look, pleased that she had come up with a quick answer. "And I'd appreciate your not making fun of my friends," she added. "Especially since you don't know them."

"I don't have to," her father said mildly. "Come here, you can give me a kiss goodbye."

Jill kissed him and called goodbye to her mother who was still upstairs. "See you later."

She was the first one to arrive at the headquarters. Jill

could see all the arm bands and banners piled up inside, and she waited impatiently outside the door for someone to come along with the keys. In a few minutes she was joined by some other volunteers, young couples with small children in tow. Jill watched the families with a pang of envy, especially a stocky young woman with a slender, intellectual-looking husband, three little girls, and a grandmother. To her it was marvelous that a whole family, three generations, came out together to take a stand against nuclear power. She felt badly that neither of her parents, nor a close friend like Diane, was with her. Not even Toby. Suddenly she was overwhelmed by Toby's desertion, and wondered how she could have thought for a minute that she could forgive him. She was grateful to him, yes, since she might never have been there if it hadn't been for him, but she would never really accept what he had done.

Pat Foner came running down the street, waving the keys and breathlessly apologizing for being late. Soon the place was a hubbub of excitement with people coming in to pick up banners and placards and arm bands. The march was to start from in front of the firehouse, as it had before. Walking there with a group of demonstrators, Jill quickly lost her sense of aloneness. She wasn't alone, and if the people she was closest to weren't with her, she would have to make new friends. Before Jill had thought of Pat and the antinuke group only as girls and boys with whom she had a limited, narrow bond. Toby had been the only one she had felt close to. But now, having come back on her own, Jill became interested in developing her friendship with them further, and made up her mind to do something about it.

She hung back from the crowd headed for the firehouse until she saw Pat approaching, then fell into step beside her. She wanted to be friendly but she couldn't think of anything to say. Finally she blurted out, "Have you seen Toby lately?"

"Not much. He's been so busy working." Then she laughed. "We'll be picketing him today. That'll be weird, won't it?"

"I never thought of that," Jill said. "I wonder how that'll make him feel."

"Not too good I guess. I wonder how he really feels working there."

"I thought it was awful. I'll never understand how he could do it."

Pat glanced at her. "Unfortunately not everyone is pure. If you're going to hang around activists you'll find out that a lot of them come and go. There's always a good hard core of people who work and stick with it, but not everyone. Life interferes. Like Toby, some have to take jobs for the same people we're against—guys who hated the war went to fight in Vietnam because not everyone could avoid it who wanted to." Pat shook her head sadly. "It can be disappointing."

"I was certainly disappointed in Toby," Jill admitted.

"I know you were. That's why we didn't see you any-more, isn't it?"

Jill nodded. "I'm ashamed to say so, but yes."

Pat patted her arm. "Don't be ashamed. I'm glad you changed your mind. We need you."

Jill gave Pat a grateful smile. "I'm glad too."

In spite of the heat, a good-sized crowd gathered, and as the demonstrators formed into a line and started to march, Jill thought that there were more people along the sidewalks cheering them on. The movement had gathered momentum over the summer, and she felt hopeful that they were making an impact. Perhaps that plant would actually never be completed.

As they approached the construction site, Jill felt her heart beating rapidly. What if Toby was there, inside the fence, watching them go by?

When they came alongside the gates, some of the construction workers jeered. "Don't take our jobs away," others yelled. "Go home." The marchers just waved to them and kept walking.

Then Jill spied Toby. He looked sweaty and hot in his work clothes, and she saw him leave what he had been doing and come to the iron gate. She couldn't fathom the expression on his face as he watched them walk by.

Suddenly he dropped the tool he had been holding and threw his hard hat on the ground. Jill stepped out of the line to see what he was doing. She saw him hoist himself up and climb the six-foot gate. "Hey you," someone behind him yelled. "What you doing, man? You crazy?"

But Toby was scaling the fence and once astride the top, he jumped to the ground. A few people watching him cheered. His face was scarlet. He saw Jill, and with a wide smile he came alongside her. "Aren't you going to march?"

"Yes, of course." She was too flustered to say anything more.

She started to move, and he walked beside her. He was the first one to speak. "I just couldn't stand being on the other side. It was too much." He glanced at her sideways. "I didn't do it for you. I hadn't planned it. Just when I saw all these people, I knew I had to be with them."

Still she couldn't talk. She didn't know what to say.

"This is what I believe," Toby said, "and I guess there's no way to compromise on that. I don't expect you to stand up and cheer, but for Christ's sake, say something, can't you?" He tried to see her face.

Jill turned around and met his eyes. "Your face is dirty," she said. "It's all smeared." Then she smiled.

Toby ran his hand over his face. "Is that all you have to say?" When he saw that she was laughing, he broke into a smile and then laughed with her.

They walked side by side for a few blocks. Then she turned to him. "Here," she said, handing him the sign she had been holding, "you carry this poster."

He took it, and gave her a meek glance. "Yes, ma'am. Anything you say."

She turned to him with a serious face. "No, it's not what I say or you say. It's what we each say ourselves. In the beginning, when you asked me to be your girl, remember, you said we had things to learn from each other. I didn't know what you meant then, and I'm not sure you did either."

"It was just a feeling I had," he replied.

"I know. But your feeling was right. We did have things to learn. We're different people, Toby, and we'll have agreements and disagreements; but I've been doing a lot of thinking. I think we still have things to learn from each other." She glanced at him sideways.

He took hold of her arm with his free hand. "Is that your way of saying you're still my girl?"

"Do you want me to be?"

"Are you kidding? But I'm no superman, you know. I'm just an ordinary guy. I may never get to Yale—if I do it'll have to be a year from now, and I may have to settle for less. A different kind of compromise. And I still have to face my father after this. What I'm saying is you're not getting the hero you were looking for. I don't want you to be disappointed again."

Jill turned around to look him full in the face. "Of course I'm going to be disappointed, so what? Life isn't perfect, you aren't perfect, and neither am I. But I'm not sorry I thought you were super, maybe someday you will be." She gave him a wry smile. "There's always hope."

Toby's hand found hers. "My instincts were right

about you in the beginning. I knew you weren't dumb."

Jill laughed. "I was dumb enough to think you *were* perfect."

"That wasn't dumb, that was blind love."

"I'll say it was." They looked at each other and laughed.

"It's better this way," Toby said, and Jill agreed.

Hila Colman was born and grew up in New York City, where she went to Calhoun School. After graduation, she attended Radcliffe College. Before she started writing for herself, she wrote publicity material and ran a book club. Her first story was sold to the *Saturday Evening Post,* and since then her stories and articles have appeared in many periodicals. Some have been dramatized for television. In 1957, she turned to writing books for teenage girls. One of them, *The Girl From Puerto Rico,* was given a special citation by the Child Study Association of America.

Mrs. Colman lives in Bridgewater, Connecticut, and has two sons.